BRUTALITY/ DIVORCE

TWO PLAYS BY GUSTAVO OTT
Translated by Heather L. McKay

ALSO BY GUSTAVO OTT AVAILABLE FROM MAGGOTS

PLAYS AND PREJUDICE –Two Plays
Your Molotov Kisses/ Two Loves and a Creature

THE LIPSTICK PLAYS – Three Plays
The Most Boring Man in the World/ Miss and Madame/ Who Ever Said I Was a Good Girl?

THE PERVERSITY PLAYS –Three Plays
80 Teeth, 4 Feet & 500 Pounds/ Chat/ Passport

THE CATASTROPHE PLAYS –Three Plays
Three Five-Dog Nights/ Juanita Claxton/ 120 Lives a Minute

DIVORCÉES, EVANGELISTS AND VEGETARIANS
(Divorciadas, evangélicas y vegetarianas)
(Bilingual Edition)

LA FOTO / THE PHOTO
(Bilingual Edition)

MUMMIES, IMMIGRANTS AND BASEBALL
Three Plays
Mummy in the Closet/ The Very Thought of You// The 8-Day Hustle

In Paperback or Kindle at Amazon.com

BRUTALITY/ DIVORCE

TWO PLAYS BY GUSTAVO OTT
Translated by Heather L. McKay

Maggots Publishers, LLC
Virginia, EE.UU.

Original Title:
Brutality
Copyright ©2016 by Gustavo Ott
All Rights Reserved.
Brutality, ©2018
© *Heather L. McKay* © *Gustavo Ott*

Original Title:
Divorcio
Copyright ©2015 by Gustavo Ott
All Rights Reserved.
Divorce, ©2017
© *Heather L. McKay* © *Gustavo Ott*

BRUTALITY/ DIVORCE, *©2018*
Two Plays by Gustavo Ott /Translated by Heather L. McKay
Maggots Publishers LLC, Virginia, USA
email: maggotsediciones@yahoo.com
COVER by Iván González
PHOTO from the Costa Rican National Theatre Company
World Premiere, San José, 2018.
Photo Design: Noé Arias

Content

Brutality/ 7
Divorce/ 103
Gustavo Ott/ 199
Heather L. McKay/ 201

BRUTALITY

"You feel the shame, humiliation, and anger at being just
another victim of prejudice, and at the same time, there's
the nagging worry that maybe... you're just no good."
Nina Simone

"Picket lines and picket signs
Don't punish me with brutality
Talk to me, so you can see
Oh, what's going on"
Marvin Gaye

Brutality won the II Aguijon/ Instituto Cervantes Playwriting Theater Award (Chicago, 2017) and was premiered by the Costa Rican National Theatre Company on April 26, 2018, in the Teatro de La Aduana, San Jose, directed by Mabel Marín. The cast was as follows:

Elías Jiménez............*Robert Glenn*
Tatiana Zamora..........*Sophia Glenn*
Aysha Morales...........*Selena Reynolds*
Javier Montenegro......*Ethan McKeeman*
Mar Jiménez.............*Katie Keller*
Laura Alvarado.........*Muna Sayeh*
William Solano..........*José Espinoza*

Jennifer Cob.............*Set Design*
Giovanni Sandí..........*Lighting Design*
Rolando Trejos.........*Costumes*
Glendon Ramírez......*Music*

Characters:

Robert Glenn, 45
Sophia Glenn, 41
Selena Reynolds, 28
Muna Sayeh, 25
Jose Espinoza, 32
Ethan McKeeman, 16
Katie Keller, 16

GUSTAVO OTT

ACT I

1/ KITCHEN

(ROBERT, in a bathrobe, is preparing breakfast. Beside him, SOPHIE, in her school bus driver's uniform.)

ROBERT: I don't see him studying, sweetheart. He gets home from school, sits in front of the TV and while he's watching, he's on his phone and his tablet. One day I went over to see who he was talking to. It wasn't just one person. He had five windows open! Girls, guys, all talking at the same time. It's crazy.

SOPHIE: Did you hear what he was saying? You know he doesn't like that.

ROBERT: No, of course not. He had earphones in and he was just laughing.

SOPHIE: Still, that can't be the reason.

ROBERT: That's not the reason? Wasting his time isn't the reason he's doing poorly in school? Not studying isn't a sign that something's wrong with your grades? I don't know, sweetheart, but I'd say it is.

SOPHIE: Maybe he's like me. I didn't study much but I still did well in school.

ROBERT: Of course you studied!

SOPHIE: No, really, not at all.

ROBERT: And you got good grades?

SOPHIE: Not good grades, no, but I did fine.

ROBERT: Not me. I had to study, a lot. I worked super hard. Incredibly hard. I'd get tired, I'd sweat I studied so much. When I went to bed it was like I'd run seven miles straight. My bones, my muscles, my head, everything hurt. I studied like an animal, like my life depended on it. And in the end, I did horrible on my tests.

SOPHIE: It's not how hard, it's the way you study, sugar.

ROBERT: I guess so. They never showed me how to study.

SOPHIE: Don't be silly. You're very smart, of course you know how to study. You're just getting old, is all. *(Calling out)* Alex, breakfast is almost ready! *(To Robert)* What about you?

ROBERT: What about me?

SOPHIE: Are you going to work?

ROBERT: Why are you asking that? *(She points out the obvious. He notices.)* You see? When have I ever forgotten to get ready for work?

SOPHIE: I told you: you're getting old. Senile.

ROBERT: Keep fucking around.

SOPHIE: Yesterday I read how age-related diseases afflict white folks like you before women like me.

ROBERT: "White folks like me?" Aren't you white? What do you think you are? Creole?

SOPHIE: I mean we southern women have more color.

ROBERT: Give me a break, you're so pale your moles shine like psychedelic ladybugs.

SOPHIE: But I've got more color than you, accept it.

ROBERT: Because you suntan. What you've got are spots from your accident, plain and simple.

SOPHIE: *(Serious)* Seriously, are you going to work today?

ROBERT: Of course, Sophie, just like every day.

SOPHIE: Since you said they suspended you starting today…

(Robert takes off his bathrobe and quickly puts on pants and a shirt. Then he grabs his police sergeant's uniform jacket.)

ROBERT: Yeah, suspended with half pay, but if I don't go in I lose that half too.

SOPHIE: Don't exaggerate.

ROBERT: I'm not exaggerating. I'm under investigation. I'm not doing anything all day, but I have to go.

SOPHIE: Sitting behind a desk is better than driving a school bus full of teenage animals for two hours. Besides, your half pay is like my whole one, so don't complain.

ROBERT: I'm not complaining. I've always said your job is more dangerous than mine.

(They prepare to leave.)

SOPHIE: How do I look?

ROBERT: White.

SOPHIE: Idiot. *(Calling out)* Alex; your food's on the table. We're leaving now! *(To Robert)* If he keeps getting bad grades maybe he can be a cop.

ROBERT: You're killing me with laughter. Have a good day, hon.

SOPHIE: You too, sugar.

(They kiss. Music.)

2/ BUS

(SOPHIE, in the driver's seat, waiting in the school bus. With her, two students: KATIE and MCKEEMAN.)

KATIE: Tell him, Sophie, tell him!

SOPHIE: But you already told him, didn't you?

KATIE: He doesn't believe me.

SOPHIE: Well, that's his problem.

KATIE: Come on, tell him. Tell him.

SOPHIE: It's no big deal, Katie. I'll tell him tomorrow. The other kids will be here soon.

KATIE: They're going to be a while. There's a meeting with the principal today.

SOPHIE: What about?

MCKEEMAN: They're probably having a talk with the students, stupid stuff.

SOPHIE: About the graffiti?

MCKEEMAN: Yeah, that shit. They're all freaking out over some stupid graffiti.

SOPHIE: Will they be long?

KATIE: They said five minutes extra. Come on, tell him, Sophie, tell him.

SOPHIE: But… what do you want me to tell him?

KATIE: About the Association you go to…

MCKEEMAN: Do you really go to that group?

KATIE: She goes to the "Struck by Lightning Association."

SOPHIE: "The Lightning Strike and Electric Shock Survivors Association," to be exact.

KATIE: Literally! The Struck by Lightning Association!

SOPHIE: (*Laughing*) I guess you could call it that. It's like Alcoholics Anonymous, but with lightning. We meet every other week.

MCKEEMAN: And you were really struck by lightning?

SOPHIE: I nearly died, but here I am.

(*SOPHIE pushes up her sleeve and shows them a lightning tattoo. KATIE and MCKEEMAN are into it.*)

MCKEEMAN/KATIE: Tell! Tell! Tell!

SOPHIE: Two years ago I was in my front yard watering the plants when all of a sudden this huge light swallowed me up. I passed out and like a half hour later I woke up, only thirty feet away from where I was before. My back hurt, not because of the lightning, because I hit a tree when I went flying. My shoes melted.

MCKEEMAN/KATIE: Wow!! Wild! Melted!

SOPHIE: I have white spots and I lost a bunch of teeth too. (*Shows them her teeth, though she's had them replaced with prosthetics)* They still hurt when the sun is really bright. And look... *(Shows them a burn on her neck)*

KATIE: That's where the lightning hit you?

SOPHIE: It was a necklace. Completely melted. I had to have surgery to get the incrusted metal back out.

MCKEEMAN: But, don't people die from that? How'd you survive?

SOPHIE: Luck. The electricity travels through your body in microseconds but if it's real fast, it doesn't necessarily kill you. Though it has its after-effects. *(The teens wait for an explanation.)* I have some depression and chronic pain that I take pills for.

MCKEEMAN: Oxy?

SOPHIE: *(Nods)* Prescription, of course. Honestly, I want to quit seeing doctors. They don't know anything. Nobody cares about post-electrocution syndrome. If it wasn't for the pills, I'd've stopped going already.

MCKEEMAN: So, do you have any extra Oxy?

KATIE: I wish I'd get struck by lightning!

SOPHIE: Don't be stupid, Katie, it hurts like hell.

KATIE: But I'd have the tattoo.

MCKEEMAN: And the Oxy.

SOPHIE: Well, you can buy Oxy on the street. And Katie, you can get a tattoo without having to risk getting fried to a crisp.

KATIE: But I want the experience.

SOPHIE: Then, don't worry, it can happen.

KATIE: Seriously?

SOPHIE: Of course. Orlando is the world capital of people struck by lightning. You live in the right place.

KATIE: Cool!

MCKEEMAN: You know what it goes for on the street?

SOPHIE: What?

MCKEEMAN: Oxy. You know what it goes for? Forty, fifty a pop.

SOPHIE: Really? So I've got a fortune in my bathroom.

MCKEEMAN: If you need to sell, let me know. I can place it for you.

SOPHIE: At that price? *(MCKEEMAN nods.)* I'll bring it tomorrow. Ok? *(We hear people coming.)* Here come the kids, we're off. By the way, guys, keep this under wraps. If the school finds out I could lose my job.

KATIE: Over the pills?

SOPHIE: All three of us would go to jail for that. I meant about being in treatment for lightning and not reporting it. They'd fire me.

MCKEEMAN/KATIE: Absolute secret!

(Music)

3/ SCHOOL

(KATIE and MCKEEMAN behind the school. To one side, a door and sign: "Orlando High. Service Entrance.")

MCKEEMAN: He's paying me 80 a pop and buying all of it. No questions asked.

KATIE: So who is he?

MCKEEMAN: His name's Nick. He's living with us.

KATIE: With your mom? I mean, he's sleeping with your mom?

MCKEEMAN: He sleeps on the couch. Maybe they're having sex and don't want me to know. I don't know. Truth is, one time I got up for a midnight snack and I didn't see him on the couch.

KATIE: Would it bother you if they are?

MCKEEMAN: No way. Nick's a special guy.

KATIE: But, are you sure his story is true?

MCKEEMAN: We checked it all out before we let him move in. We're not idiots.

KATIE: The guy came from the future. Wooow!

MCKEEMAN: Exactly. He came from the future to tell us something really important. Check this, when he got here he didn't recognize the city, or our house, which belongs to his current family, only they don't live there yet. They will in two hundred years!

KATIE: Two hundred years! So, he comes from…

MCKEEMAN: From 2216. And he says by then the United States won't exist.

KATIE: We're going to disappear!

MCKEEMAN: That in 2216 it's all foreigners. We'll speak Spanish and white people are persecuted by the Latino, black and foreign majority.

KATIE: Unbelievable!

MCKEEMAN: Nick came from the future to warn us and to do something about it.

KATIE: Is that why you painted that picture on the wall?

MCKEEMAN: It's not random graffiti. It's a really common symbol in 2216. Of the White Resistance; fighters who cross the border or scale the wall from Canada to repopulate and finally return to the United States of America.

KATIE: But maybe we should stop the graffiti, McKeeman. They're looking for us and if I get expelled I don't know what I'll do. Dad said he was going to draw and quarter me.

MCKEEMAN: Don't worry. He'll make you get a job. That's what Mom said too: if I do bad in school, I'll have to get a job.

KATIE: That's not so bad.

MCKEEMAN: Of course not. You make bank.

KATIE: You buy whatever you want.

MCKEEMAN Like, supplies to stock our hideout and prepare for the coming wars. *(KATIE loves the idea and kisses him. Beat)* This morning I sent an anonymous note to the principal about Sophie, the bus driver.

KATIE: About the lightning? *(MCKEEMAN nods.)* Are you nuts? Why'd you do that? They'll fire her!

MCKEEMAN: The bitch never brought me the Oxy. And I'd placed it with Nick.

KATIE: The guy from the future's the one dealing Oxy?

MCKEEMAN: Of course. We're gonna use that money to finance the first cell of the Anti-Appropriation Militias. We have to make money so we can change the future. So that 2216 belongs to us too.

KATIE: I thought you wanted the money to go to the Zombie Harpies concert.

MCKEEMAN: That too. Not everything's about liberating our race, right?

(MCKEEMAN quickly sketches the symbol of the White Resistance in 2216. Then they hear a noise from behind the door.)

MCKEEMAN: Here he comes!

KATIE: Fuck, remember don't kill him.

MCKEEMAN : Of course not.

KATIE: We're not damn murderers.

MCKEEMAN: What if he's got a gun?

KATIE: That guy? He doesn't even have papers! What kind of gun is he gonna have?

MCKEEMAN: You don't need papers, Katie.

KATIE: You don't?

MCKEEMAN: Look. *(Pulls out a Glock. KATIE is surprised.)* You order it online and boom. Anyone can do it.

(Just then the door opens and out comes JOSE ESPINOZA. He waves to the teens and walks off.)

MCKEEMAN: *(To KATIE, holding up a baseball bat)* Ready?

KATIE: *(Also with a bat. Kisses him.)* Ready, baby.

(KATIE and MCKEEMAN run after JOSE ESPINOZA. Music.)

4/ SELENA'S OFFICE

(JUAN ESPINOZA, beaten up, is sitting on a couch. SELENA paces back and forth.)

SELENA: It's not a test; it's a list of questions to legalize your status. She told me it's easy, Jose. A cinch, she said. It won't even be in English!

JOSE E: I can speak English.

SELENA: Yes, of course, I know that.

JOSE E: And the girl? She's Arab?

SELENA: Lebanese.

JOSE E: Those Lebanese are really shrewd. Where I'm from there's lots of them and they're all well off. How old is your friend?

SELENA: Her name is Muna and she's 25.

JOSE E: See? She's young. Young people know more.

SELENA: Jose, you're young too and you'll do fine. The problem's going to be the other matter...

JOSE E: What other matter?

SELENA: You know perfectly well what I mean.

JOSE E: But it just happened a few days ago. Maybe they haven't gotten the information yet.

SELENA: That's what we're hoping for. Though it would be an ethical breach if I don't tell them everything I know about you.

JOSE E: Then tell them, Dr. Selena.

SELENA: Just Selena.

JOSE E: Tell them everything, Mrs. Selena.

SELENA: Miss.

JOSE E: Since you're a lawyer.

SELENA: Call me Selena that's all.

JOSE E: Selena that's all. *(She looks at him in disapproval. JOSE laughs.)* Selena, I just don't want you to get in trouble for helping me.

SELENA: If only you hadn't gotten so much attention!

JOSE E: I tried to make it perfect.

SELENA: But it wasn't perfect, Jose. It was never going to be. Disguising yourself as an African American to elude immigration officers. Really?

JOSE E: Dr. Selena, I couldn't think of anything else and besides I had no choice. I saw myself in the mirror and I looked real beat up. Those kids at the school got me good. I had bruises everywhere, I still do. Whenever I went out people kept staring at me so much and I got scared. If normal people were looking at me that much, ICE was going to stop me for sure. They'd think I was some kind of criminal without papers, a troublemaker, a bad guy. So, decided to do it.

SELENA: And it didn't occur to you that you'd stick out even more?

JOSE E: No, of course not. I rubbed on shoe polish, I walked like them, talked like them. I even put baking soda on my teeth so they'd shine like theirs.

SELENA: Like ours, you mean. *(Noting that he doesn't understand)* I'm African-American, Jose!

JOSE E: No, I didn't know. You don't look black.

SELENA: Good God! What color do you think this is?

JOSE E: Like where I'm from.

SELENA: Exactly: black.

JOSE E: Maybe since you're a woman you don't look…

SELENA: Jose, you need to stop talking right now. That's sexist, racist, misogynist. The whole menu!

JOSE E: I swear I'm none of those things. In my country I was always very respectful.

SELENA: But here you need to learn to watch what you say.

JOSE E: Is my English bad?

SELENA: No, but some of the things you say! And dressing up as an African American doesn't help any, Jose.

JOSE E: Really? I just didn't realize. All I wanted was to stop being Jose Espinoza and become Jack Black, for safety is all.

SELENA: *(SELENA, giving in, laughs)* And Black, no less. You're a disaster, Jose.

JOSE E: You have such a pretty laugh.

SELENA: The first person who saw you noticed you were painted black, that you weren't real. And then the second, and the security guard too, and by the time the police got there they were all laughing at you.

JOSE E: It's just they were asking everyone who looked Latino for papers and I...

SELENA: It's called Profiling and all of us who aren't white in this country get caught in it. You see the difference?

JOSE E: Maybe. But with a different skin color, for a few minutes anyway, I felt safe.

(SELENA sits beside him.)

SELENA: If my brothers heard you, or the pastor, they'd crack up. As a black man you felt safe from the police! Are you serious?

JOSE E: I could've gone on like that forever and been happy.

SELENA: With them laughing at you!

JOSE E: Yes, but safe.

(SELENA laughs again. JOSE tries to kiss her. She pulls away, alarmed.)

SELENA: What was that?

JOSE E: I...

SELENA: You have a wife, Jose!

JOSE E: Excuse me, it was a moment...

SELENA: A moment?

JOSE E: There's nothing wrong with a moment.

SELENA: There's nothing wrong with a kiss? You told me you're getting your papers in order for her and your kids, to bring them all here!

JOSE E: Yes, but you just have such a pretty laugh, doctor.

SELENA: But I'm not flirting with you, Jose. You understand that? Right?

JOSE E: I've only been in this country one year and you're the only person who's been nice to me. Excuse me, doctor. I won't do it again.

SELENA: Of course you won't do it again. And I'm not a doctor, I'm a lawyer.

JOSE E: In El Salvador we call lawyers doctor.

SELENA: Well, you're not there anymore. You're here. And if you want to be legal in the United States, understand that you can't try to kiss, or touch women, just because they're nice. Happiness and good manners don't equal a sexual proposition, Jose. And don't change your race again, or use words that offend other people. Understand?

JOSE E: *(Ashamed. He holds his arm, which hurts.)* Yes, of course. I have a lot to learn.

SELENA: Does it still hurt?

JOSE E: It's nothing. It's going away.

SELENA: Your pain pills?

JOSE E: I'm taking them.

SELENA: Really? You're not selling them?

JOSE E: A few. Not many. *(SELENA gestures "this is the limit.")* I had a debt that couldn't wait. Getting papers is expensive, you yourself told me the price.

SELENA: Jose! Jose! My God! How many times are you going to break the law before you get accepted in this country? Do you really want to be in pain to get your papers?

JOSE E: The pain is nothing. It means nothing. But papers do, doctor. Besides, I've had pain all my life. And if they'll pay that much for those pills on the street, what do you want? I say let it keep hurting. There are things that hurt worse and you don't get pills for them, let me tell you.

SELENA: I can lower the costs, that's the least important thing, but you take care of that pain, Jose. Ok? Do it for me at least. If I know you're selling your pills to pay for the process, I won't be able to keep doing my job. *(Beat)* And the kids who beat you up? Have you seen them again? Are they still at school?

JOSE E: Yeah, they're still there. One of them has a gun.

SELENA: A gun?

JOSE E: Of course. And I'm terrified of them, doctor. Terrified.

5/ BAR/NIGHTCLUB

(SELENA is waiting at a bar in a bar/nightclub. She looks around at everyone happily, glad to be there. Suddenly, her face lights up more. MUNA arrives.)

SELENA: You didn't have a hard time?

MUNA: A wrong turn, but then the rest was fine.

SELENA: *(Gesturing to the place)* What do you think?

MUNA: Nice. Nice. There's so many young people!

SELENA: We're young, Muna.

MUNA: Of course, but in Lebanon this couldn't happen.

SELENA: Young people drinking and dancing?

MUNA: A gay bar.

SELENA: Don't label it, Muna. Treat it like a regular place. People dance, talk, hook up, like at any other place in the world.

MUNA: Don't say that, Selena. That world you're talking about is tiny. In Beirut not only are there no gay bars, there are no bars. Period. And meeting places aren't even allowed for women, so you can imagine.

SELENA: I thought Lebanon was more open than the other countries over there, isn't it?

MUNA: A little more than the other caves dominated by hairy guys and their prayers. But don't forget, in our world a society that's open on the outside has a hairy guy on the inside.

SELENA: *(Orders a drink)* Here you don't have to worry about hairy guys. Or hairy girls, though there are some real hotties.

MUNA: *(Flirtatious)* Which one?

SELENA: Like her.

MUNA: *(Looking at her)* Gorgeous.

SELENA: Gorgeous. Like you, Muna. So forget Beirut, which sounds like the name of a Sundance movie by the way, and have one of these mojitos with me. This Cuban girl makes them world class.

MUNA: *(Takes the drink)* Beirut? I wouldn't remember it even if it had a Disney name. Consider it forgotten. In any case, now that I'm getting so forgetful, it's perfect timing.

SELENA: Forgetful? Really?

MUNA: Yeah. Like it was a disease.

SELENA: Don't say that, honey. I'm sure it's nothing. The change of scenery; one thing affects the other. That's all.

MUNA: Like yesterday I forgot where my phone was.

SELENA: Muna: Everyone forgets where they leave their phone!

MUNA: I'm talking about my home phone, the one that's always been in the same place.

SELENA: Don't stress. You're 25. A girl forgets the little things. You've got a Samsung, so of course you're going to forget that prehistoric thing, which looks like a faded flowerpot, by the way. *(Seductive)* Want to dance?

MUNA: Not yet.

SELENA: One day you're gonna have to try it, Muna. Remember you're a legal resident now.

MUNA: Yeah, of course, but I feel embarrassed today.

SELENA: Because you're at a gay bar?

MUNA: That and...

SELENA: Because you don't know how to dance.

MUNA: نظرتم الليلة جميلة جدا، ولكن أنا لم تحرك جسدي في خمسة و عشرين عاما 1

SELENA: What? *(Muna laughs. Takes a drink.)* I'm going to learn to speak Arabic and then you'll see!

(They both laugh, seductive)

MUNA: I said people here dance like they're getting zapped by electricity.

SELENA: That's how we shake off the stress of the work week.

MUNA: I guess that's why they named this nightclub "Pulse."

---

[1] *"You're really beautiful tonight, but understand I haven't moved my body in twenty-five years."/ "'ant jamilat hadhih allaylat , lkn 'atfahum 'anani lm naqul jusdiin khilal khms weshryn eamana. "*

SELENA: (Moving closer) Because it makes your heart beat faster.

MUNA: Do people kiss in all bars or just in these?

SELENA: In these and all of them.

MUNA: I like kisses.

(They kiss.)

MUNA: Yeah, I like long kisses and eyes closed.

(Music)

6/ RESTAURANT

(ROBERT, in his police uniform, in a restaurant. Across from him, SOPHIE. In the distance, we see other cops having lunch there too.)

SOPHIE: Suspended.

ROBERT: Suspended? But, why?

SOPHIE: They gave me a two-week suspension. It becomes permanent if I don't turn in my medical report.

ROBERT: Over the lightning? Is that it? How'd they find out?

SOPHIE: My own carelessness. I told a couple of kids and...

ROBERT: You're so stupid, Sophie! An idiot! Why in the world would you tell them that?

SOPHIE: Robert, people talk about themselves. Someone asks, there's a silence and you talk. You told me yours.

ROBERT: I was forced to by an Internal Affairs Commission, then I had to file a report that went public and after that the media ran the story over and over again... I didn't tell out of the goodness of my heart. It was a national scandal. You did it not because you had to, but because there was a silence. You're a moron.

SOPHIE: Well, it's done. I felt the need to talk to someone about it and I did. What do you want me to say? The kids on the bus treat me like an idiot and I thought if they knew what had happened to me, what I've been through, what I really am, they'd respect me more.

ROBERT: (*Annoyed, pushes his food away*) I don't know what we'll do if you lose your job, Sophie.

SOPHIE: What's done is done.

ROBERT: At least my suspension should be over soon.

SOPHIE: How long do we have to wait till they reinstate you at full pay?

ROBERT: After today's testimony, it could be two or three weeks. That's what they said. Though they told me the victim's family could bring two more charges and then the whole thing will take longer and…Damnit!

SOPHIE: Two more charges! What do those thugs want? To crucify you?! The police have no one to defend them, that's for sure.

ROBERT: It's the media. And the protests, the organizations.

SOPHIE: If the guy wasn't black, there wouldn't have been such an uproar.

ROBERT: But he was.

SOPHIE: If a white cop shoots another white guy, four shots, the way you did, there wouldn't be all this press, or pressure, or suspensions, or police brutality. If you say accident, that's what it is.

ROBERT: That's not the problem, Sophie. The problem is, black or white, without my job and without yours, the numbers don't add up.

SOPHIE: What are we going to do?

ROBERT: First we have to talk to Alex. Tell him we have to tighten our belts. He's supposed to start college soon but we have to tell him the truth.

SOPHIE: The truth is going to kill him.

ROBERT: Doesn't it always? But the truth is the truth, the truth will set you free, and the truth is he doesn't have the grades to get a scholarship and we don't have the big bucks for him to go to college. Now even less. We don't even have enough for his food! So we tell him the truth: that he should wait and get a job first... *(Notices that SOPHIE suddenly isn't paying attention)* Are you listening to me? What's wrong with you?

SOPHIE: *(Talking softly)* Don't look.

ROBERT: What's going on?

SOPHIE: That guy there.

ROBERT: Which one?

SOPHIE: Sitting alone, with a hamburger...

ROBERT: The black guy. Yeah.

SOPHIE: Look between his legs.

ROBERT: You're looking between some guy's legs, Sophie?

SOPHIE: Stupid, look what he's got between his legs!

ROBERT: *(Looking)* He must have his zipper down and he's flashing his...!

SOPHIE: No, Robert. I think it's something else.

ROBERT: *(Realizing)* Fuck! That's the end of a rifle! It looks like the muzzle of an AR-15!

SOPHIE: Oh my god, oh my god, oh my god. All these cops eating here and we're the only ones who notice!

ROBERT: *(Pulls out his phone)* I'm going to call headquarters to put out an alert.

SOPHIE: Do you have your gun on you?

ROBERT: Yes, of course. I'm in uniform!

SOPHIE: I'm asking because I don't want you playing the hero. Got it? You're not leaving me an unemployed widow raising a teenage son who doesn't even want to talk to her. Besides, you're already under investigation for killing that other black asshole!

ROBERT: Then, what do you want me to do?

SOPHIE: Nothing. We get up and we leave. Let someone else deal with this mess, with investigations and suspensions. You can't take any more.

ROBERT: Fine. You go first then, like you're going to make a call. And when you're outside, run.

SOPHIE: What about you?

ROBERT: I'll go to the bathroom, casual, and raise the alarm from there.

SOPHIE: I'm scared.

ROBERT: Don't be. Nothing's going to happen.

(SOPHIE gets up, nervous. Suddenly we hear something fall on the floor and a voice shouting.)

VOICE: I'm sick of all this police brutality against my brothers! And that's why I came here today, to kill all the white cops I can!

(Music)

7/A ZOMBIE HARPIES CONCERT

(Standing, listening to the band, MCKEEMAN and KATIE. Sometimes they're pushed by the huge wave of the mosh pit, which they love.)

MCKEEMAN: That's the bassist! Look at him! He's the best in the world!

KATIE: How do you know he's the best in the world?

MCKEEMAN: It's what the experts say, Katie. The Zombie Harpies bassist is the best in the world.

KATIE: There are experts who say who's the best bassist?

MCKEEMAN: He's the best bassist in the world and the drummer, get a good look, 'cause he's the best in the world too.

KATIE: The two best in the same band!

MCKEEMAN: And the guitarist is one of the best.

KATIE: What about the singer?

MCKEEMAN: The singer's shit.

KATIE: Did the experts prove that too?

MCKEEMAN: Totally.

KATIE: Whatever, the important thing is that you like them, baby. Look! *(She lifts her shirt, shows him her back. She has a lightning bolt tattoo.)*

MCKEEMAN: Woooow! Did you get hit by lightning?

KATIE: Not yet. It all depends on you. *(Kisses him, very passionately.)*

MCKEEMAN: *(Shouts, thrilled)* Coming to the Harpies concert with you is my biggest dream come truuuuuue!

(The wave of people comes and sweeps them along. They laugh and kiss.)

MCKEEMAN: Katie…Katie…Katie… you're the lightning bolt that splits me in two. What if we get married?

KATIE: What?

MCKEEMAN: What if we get married.

KATIE: Just like that.

MCKEEMAN: Well, we do everything together. And you want to get hit by lightning…

KATIE: That's not a reason to get married, McKeeman.

MCKEEMAN: Thing is…thing is… Nick. Mom's boyfriend? You know?

KATIE: The guy from the future. From 2216, right?

MCKEEMAN: Right. 2216. Nick said I'm in the history books of the future when they talk about the Race Battles. That's what he said.

KATIE: What Race Battles?

MCKEEMAN: These super famous social struggles that are coming up. And he said the history books in 2216 say I'm one of the first instigators. That my fight is considered the precedent for the Historic Resistance, he said that, the Great Historic Resistance. You see? Of white people. Of us. And the most interesting part, the best part out of all the stuff he told me, is that those history books also say I married a woman named Katie. The book says that; Katie.

KATIE: Maybe it's some other Katie…

MCKEEMAN: It's you: a tall, blonde, white woman who I knew since I was young, my first love and all, and you help me keep my emotional balance, you were something like the co-author of all my exploits in the first movement of the Great Historic Resistance against the oppression of the Unified Minorities.

KATIE: He told you that? Seriously?

MCKEEMAN: That you were my muse in the struggle. That in the future, in 2216, lots of girls are named after you, in your honor.

KATIE: In my honor! Wooow!

MCKEEMAN: And mine too. He said there's an airport for spaceships called "the McKeeman Launch Pad."

KATIE: But in 2216 there aren't any white people in the U.S.?

MCKEEMAN: The launch pad is in Canada, where the white people live after they're thrown out of the U.S. Remember? The white people sneak across the border, with the help of Wolves, or by climbing the wall the Latinos and blacks built to keep us out. And guess what.

In 2216 there's a tunnel, the biggest one, named after you!

KATIE: The Katie Keller Tunnel!

MCKEEMAN: Katie McKeeman. That's what Nick said. That why we should get married, so we don't interfere with the course of history and the Great Historic Resistance.

KATIE: But…

MCKEEMAN: He knows all about us. He told me it was all History, that kids recite it, that there are poems about it.

KATIE: Poems? So what do the poems say?

MCKEEMAN: That once, in the middle of a Zombie Harpies concert, I got down on one knee and proposed to you… *(Just then he kneels)* And that, like Nick suggested, we ran away from home and started the battle against the white holocaust. And then, even the Zombie Harpies wrote us a song. A war song. The hymn of our generation!

KATIE: Seriously? And are you sure this Nick guy came from the future?

MCKEEMAN: Katie, don't be like them.

KATIE: Them?

MCKEEMAN: People who believe in nothing. We either believe or we disappear. So? Do we interfere with the Great Historic Resistance or do you marry me?

(She looks at him. She kisses him and yells Yessssss! Another wave of people comes. They laugh, happy.

KATIE listens to the music and dances in a frenzy. Suddenly, KATIE stops and stares at the band.)

KATIE: Hey, what happened to the bassist?

MCKEEMAN: What's wrong with him?

KATIE: He fell down.

MCKEEMAN: Maybe he got electrocuted. Another one struck by lightning!

(KATIE feels a pain in her back. She touches it. It's bleeding. MCKEEMAN touches her and confirms she's hurt.)

KATIE: *(Terrified)* Baby, they're shooting.

(The band stops playing. We hear gunfire and shouting.)

8/ HALLWAY

(JOSE ESPINOZA and SELENA in the hallway of an office building. Both are dressed very nicely.)

SELENA: *(Annoyed)* Jose, what did we agree on?

JOSE E: Lots of things…I don't know, I don't know.

SELENA: Yes, you do. We agreed that the best thing was for everyone to forget your blackface episode. That after a few days everyone would forget about it, particularly the agent handling your immigration case. We agreed on that. We agreed on that.

JOSE E: Yes, we agreed on that. What's wrong?

SELENA: The interview is what's wrong, Jose! The interview you did at that TV station!

JOSE E: Oh, that. It was a local channel, doctor. No one saw it. Not even my friends heard about that interview. TV moves on and people forget.

SELENA: Well your immigration agent heard about it. You think TV disappears? Not even a little bit. It hangs on, like you were published in the paper or written on the walls. You're online! Have you heard of this secret, invisible thing called, Internet? You're there! Your idiotic photo with your stupid black face is circling the globe! And not to raise concerns about issues of immigration or race, no, so people can laugh at you. And apparently your agent, like everyone else, likes to spend his free time watching cats, accidents, and undocumented immigrant morons who try to evade ICE by wearing blackface.

JOSE E: I couldn't say no. The reporter who called me was so concerned...

SELENA: With laughing at you!

JOSE E: She wanted to help.

SELENA: And was very pretty too.

JOSE E: And she was very pretty.

SELENA: You're an idiot. A sexist idiot. They show you a skirt and you confess. And the worst part, it's your own people who do whatever they want with all of you.

JOSE E: All of us... Us who?

SELENA: You. People without papers. Terrified Hispanics. To you.

JOSE E: Selena, the TV didn't do anything. The pretty reporter didn't either. I wanted to tell my story. Not about dressing up as a black man, that's beside the point and I can see why they'd laugh at me for that. I laugh at me. But what I...

SELENA: It's not beside the point, Jose, this is racial! The tension, the violence, the inequalities, immigration! All racial! Don't forget it. It's the most important issue, the fundamental contradiction in this country: race, Jose. And you, whether you believe it or not, you're at the heart of it. Hasn't it sunk in? What country have you been living in this entire year? Because if it's the United States, you have to see immigration isn't the issue. It's race!

JOSE E: I mean that the story I told in the interview isn't about race, it's about being a victim. I was a victim, ma'am.

SELENA: Exactly, that's why I don't want you talking about how it's beside the point! *(Fed up)* A white Hispanic man wearing blackface to feel safe from the police! Do you have any idea how offensive that can be?

JOSE E: Remember, anyway, I'm still the victim here. It was the cop who started giving me funny looks, okay, maybe because of my disguise. And the first thing he said was my camouflage wasn't working. But I didn't resist, I just pretended I didn't understand, that's all. "I don't speak English," I said. We were both completely aware that the black spray I'd covered myself with wasn't working. Maybe because I didn't put shoe polish on my ears. Maybe I overdid it with darkening my hair, or the way I was walking or my facial features. I was wearing lipstick that day because I figured black people have shiny lips. I don't know, maybe I'm not so good at disguises. The cop saw me and asked for my papers. I don't know if he was immigration or security, but I didn't have any, so I took off running and I fell. The cop caught up and jammed his knee in my chest. He was yelling and while he was yelling he pushed down harder. I was suffocating. I passed out. I nearly died under that guy!

SELENA: Jose, we know that, but...

JOSE E: No, you don't know, because to you it's race and to me it's almost getting killed.

SELENA: That's what I'm trying to tell you; it's the same thing, Jose.

JOSE E: *(Goes to the window)* I understand they call it police brutality.

SELENA: Yes, police brutality, of course. But the priority for you is getting legal, getting your rights and then you can take on police brutality. Most likely your meeting with the agent today will get postponed again since, even though you're absolutely the victim, for that very reason, now they think you're hiding something.

JOSE E: I'm not hiding anything. I wasn't even hiding anything in El Salvador. *(Looking out the window)* Selena; is this a federal building?

SELENA: Yes, a federal building.

JOSE E: Are there lots of government offices here?

SELENA: Mail, taxes, there's an ATF office and on this floor there's Homeland Security. You've been here before. Why are you asking?

JOSE E: The red flag with the X on it, that's from the south…Right?

SELENA: Are there anti-immigration protestors out there? Don't worry, it happens. They know this is where they give undocumented people their papers and…

JOSE E: No, there aren't protesters. But I see a guy, he's armed, wearing fatigues, raising that southern flag. And right beside him there's two cops lying on the ground. I think he shot them.

SELENA: Seriously? *(Heads for the window)*

JOSE E: And now the guy pulled something out of an SUV and he ran off, yelling.

SELENA: *(Looking out the window)* What?

JOSE E: And that SUV. Is it his? What's he yelling?

SELENA: Jose, run, run!

JOSE E: Run? But, what about my immigration appointment?

SELENA: Run…run…!!! That SUV could be a car bomb!!!!

(We hear an enormous explosion.)

8/ BAR/NIGHTCLUB

(MUNA takes SELENA by the face, as though to kiss her, but she doesn't.)

MUNA: That has nothing to do with it, Selena.

SELENA: Maybe it does, maybe it does have something to do with it. And that's the thing. You don't see it, it's invisible to you, but it's there.

MUNA: Honey, Selena, I'm sure. I don't feel the same. It's normal. There doesn't have to be an explanation.

SELENA: Of course there has to be an explanation! Everything has one!

MUNA: Not love.

SELENA: Love most of all. *(Beat)* Just like that? Out of nowhere?

MUNA: I'm 25. It's normal. You fall in and out of love, all for no reason.

SELENA: No reason! A building falling on top of me isn't a reason?

MUNA: Of course not.

SELENA: Really?

MUNA: Really, Selena.

SELENA: Suddenly wasn't the American girl of your dreams anymore, a smiling American girl with high hopes and everything going for her. Instead I was a victim of terrorism, like you, like all the girls where you're from. Now I'm not an other to you, just one more. Isn't that a reason?

MUNA: You're dreaming up nonsense, Selena. And not every girl from my country is...

SELENA: Maybe I should be in another terrorist attack.

MUNA: Don't say that.

SELENA: Maybe then you'll love me again.

MUNA: Please, stop.

SELENA: That would be a record. To be in two terrorist attacks!

MUNA: A record? Here maybe. In my country you can be in twelve a year.

SELENA: But where a building falls on you? Don't trivialize my odyssey.

MUNA: It's not trivial. But in Beirut a building can fall on you and the sky itself can fall on you. And not even in a year, in the same month. I have a cousin who was in two attacks in the same week. A bomb at the market on Tuesday; gunfire at the café on Friday. The next Tuesday a cat crossed her path and the poor girl fell and hit her head on a stair. She spent ten days in the hospital.

SELENA: Good thing we agreed not to trivialize.

(Pause. They look away from each other. Then, SELENA, trying to see what MUNA sees, questions her.)

SELENA: Is there another woman? Is that it? Did you fall in love with another woman?

MUNA: No, of course not.

SELENA: So?

MUNA: It's just I feel like I could break.

SELENA: Because of me?

MUNA: When I leave the house, suddenly, I get the feeling that any second I'm going to shatter.

SELENA: Because of my attack? Because of my terrorist bombing?

MUNA: I think it has to do with forgetting.

SELENA: About the phone? That once you forgot your phone?

MUNA: No, I mean I started to forget you.

SELENA: Don't be an idiot!

MUNA: Really. Your name, the way you look, the things you say. Suddenly, I had to try really hard to remember you, and I thought: this can't be love, this is loneliness. Whatever, but it's not love.

SELENA: And the sex. Did you forget the sex too?

MUNA: With you, yes.

SELENA: Not with another woman?

MUNA: Not with myself. *(Kisses SELENA)* Come on, let's keep talking, keep coming here. I like Pulse. Let's have fun, that's what I want; to have fun for a couple of years, with no worries. No commitments, no plans. Falling in and out of love. Not too much desire or disdain. To live however, up against whoever, at max volume, no speed limit, knowing and unknowing in seconds. Don't you get it?

SELENA: Of course I do: you want to be free.

MUNA: Yes. Free. You should understand that better than anyone.

SELENA: Being free to be free.

MUNA: It's not so much to ask.

(But what MUNA has been watching is something else. She goes to SELENA, who thinks she's going to kiss her again.)

MUNA: *(Worried)* Honey: that guy. You see him?

SELENA: *(Disappointed)* What about him?

MUNA: He's wearing a trench coat. *(SELENA's face says "So?")* In this heat?

SELENA: Muna, there's nothing strange about it. We're at a nightclub. People dress weird.

MUNA: But he's got his hands in his pockets and a big coat. Don't you think maybe he's hiding something?

SELENA: Leave him alone. We've seen that guy here lots of times. He's a regular. He even slept with a friend of mine! He likes them black. They all do, except you, of course. Definitively, black women cannot win; not with men or with women, no matter what race they are.

MUNA: (*On her own track*) In my country if someone looks like that it's because they're planning something.

SELENA: Forget the Middle East, Muna, and live your Sundance movie.

(*Suddenly, we hear a 911 operator, loud.*)

911: 911, what's your emergency?

VOICE: (*False*) What's coming is Jihad! They'll pay for the crimes the West has committed! Long live ISIS!

911: Where are you calling from? What do you mean by…?

(*We hear the line go dead.*)

VOICE: (*With hatred, personal*) Faggots, goddamn faggots. Lesbians, and faggots. Die, all of you. We're all going to die today!

(*Music*)

END OF ACT ONE

ACT II

1/ CLASSROOM IN A PRIVATE SCHOOL

(Whiteboard, window, intercom, a drinking fountain and some cushions scattered on the floor. To one side, an area with various notices about activities. Onstage, MUNA and SOPHIE. MUNA has just arrived and is just setting her purse down on one of the tables. SOPHIE arrived earlier.)

SOPHIE: Nice to meet you. You're…?

MUNA: Muna Sayeh. From the bar. Seven months ago.

SOPHIE: I'm from the restaurant with the police.

MUNA: Yeah. I remember that was…

SOPHIE: Next week it'll be a year.

MUNA: I recognized you, of course.

SOPHIE: I get that a lot. "I know you from somewhere," like they'd seen me on signs in the grocery store.

MUNA: *(Laughing)* The same thing happens to me…

SOPHIE: Or else, "I saw you on TV the other day." And they say it with a smile like I was on some cooking show.

MUNA: But I recognized you from the TV show we were on together a couple of months ago, don't you remember?

SOPHIE: With you? *(Not remembering)* I've just been on so many...CNN?

MUNA: Yeah, with...

SOPHIE: The good looking host. White, gray hair, who knows how to talk fast.

MUNA: That's the one.

SOPHIE: Gorgeous. *(She stops at the school notice board)* But he didn't pay much attention to me. He was looking at the young girl, the one from the concert shooting. *(Reads)* "Encounter with Terrorism Victims." What a way to phrase it. I think these teachers watch too much TV. Also, it seems poorly written...

MUNA: How?

SOPHIE: Like it was referring to a sect that specializes in being victims of terrorism.

MUNA: Like it was a personality trait.

SOPHIE: *(Mimicking a teacher)* "Come right in, boys and girls, to the terrorist sideshow." *(Looking at a photo of a school bus)* I worked at a school once...

MUNA: Are you a teacher?

SOPHIE: No, a bus driver. I picked kids up and drove them and all.

MUNA: I love those yellow school buses. They hold a certain poetry, don't you think?

SOPHIE: But there's a lot of terrorism in those kids. If I told you the things they told me, the things they did while I was driving them to school or home again, it gives you goose bumps. And the way they talked! Insults, insults and that's about it.

MUNA: *(Laughs)* So they're the ones in the sideshow. Not us.

SOPHIE: But this is a private school. I've heard the terrorism here is softer. *(Reading another notice)* Listen to this: *(Reads)* "The Administration wants to remind all students that offensive graffiti in the hallways or classrooms will not be tolerated. Be aware that any students involved in these acts of vandalism will face serious repercussions." Repercussions, how scary.

MUNA: But if rich kids go here, who are they offending with their graffiti?

SOPHIE: There must be minorities. And girls too, of course. And a few wimpy kids who don't play sports and all.

MUNA: There's always someone weaker, huh?

SOPHIE: Didn't you have any in your school, there, where you came from?

MUNA: Yeah, sure. And we tortured them. We bullied the ugliest girls, and the kids with more money bullied us, and the boys bullied the girls, and the boys bullied each other over any little thing.

(Enter JOSE ESPINOZA. We hardly recognize him. He dresses and looks very different. He looks like a different man.)

JOSE E: Hi, sorry. I'm late but...

SOPHIE: Are we starting?

JOSE E: Sorry?

MUNA: Aren't you the...?

JOSE E: I'm here for the conference.

SOPHIE: Are you a victim, a reporter or just curious?

JOSE E: A victim. A victim.

SOPHIE: Where were you?

JOSE E: In the attack on the federal building.

SOPHIE: How awful! Have I seen you somewhere? Were you at the show on CNN?

MUNA: Hi, I'm Mona Sayeh.

SOPHIE: Sophie Glenn.

JOSE E: I'm Joe Spine.

MUNA: Spine?

JOSE E: When do you think we'll get started?

SOPHIE: *(Going to another school poster)* I've been on a lot of TV shows with Federal Building survivors. They never get tired of inviting you all, even if that was domestic terrorism and the issue is Islamic Radicals.

JOSE E: I guess they call it "balance."

MUNA: *(SOPHIE doesn't hear her.)* A car bombing by militias. Domestic terrorism. Of course. Now I remember! Jose Espinoza!

JOSE E: Joe…

MUNA: You were a client of a friend of mine, the lawyer…

JOSE E: Selena Reynolds?

(SOPHIE goes over to them.)

MUNA: That's her, the one who was in two attacks.

JOSE E: Yeah, some luck.

SOPHIE: Two attacks? That's nothing. First, I got hit by lightning, no less, lightning, while I was working in my yard. *(Shows her tattoo)* Then, I was on the front line in the attack on white police officers at the restaurant. And to top things off, a week ago another lightning bolt came down on me, not directly but really close, while I was waiting for a cab. And it wasn't even raining! So watch out for me.

MUNA: Or any of us!

(The three laugh.)

JOSE E: We should save these conversations for when we talk to the kids, to make them laugh at least once in a while.

MUNA: They said this class was the most interested and they've been waiting for weeks.

JOSE E: I'm guessing that's because of the TV coverage.

SOPHIE: We're sort of celebrities, shooting stars…

(They laugh again.)

MUNA: I'd rather not be so famous, at least not for what happened to me.

SOPHIE: Personally I like remembering it. I suppose it's like therapy. The attention has made these last months more bearable. And the money, which you always need to pay off your debts. People don't realize this terrorism thing comes with all sorts of financial problems…

JOSE E: What was yours again…?

SOPHIE: At the restaurant with the cops, almost a year ago. Next week we're doing a special memorial show. On CNN again.

MUNA: *(Putting things together)* Aren't you married to a police officer?

SOPHIE: We got divorced a month after the attack.

MUNA: I didn't know. I'm sorry.

SOPHIE: That's how it is. These events affect everything. Like the world had ended and all of a sudden it's remade. Divorce, splitting up, to see if something changes. The past, maybe. But nothing changes, you're more alone, that's true, but nothing changes. The terror stays the same, married, single, widowed, or divorced. Well, maybe not widowed.

MUNA: Not widowed, I'm sure.

SOPHIE: But we're still friends. We have a son, Alex, and now everything's more normal. *(MUNA tries to hug her, but SOPHIE stops her.)* It's fine. Only young people like you think divorce is a big deal. It isn't. It's like you moved. Have you ever moved?

MUNA: I'm from Lebanon.

SOPHIE: Well, then like that.

MUNA: Something like that happened to me, but the other way around. After the bombing at the federal building, my girlfriend and I started drifting apart. She was a victim in that attack.

SOPHIE: *(Trying to hold back)* Your girlfriend?

MUNA: Yeah, we were a couple. But after the building fell on her, I don't know why, but I wanted to be free.

SOPHIE: Why?

MUNA: I don't know. To live? Then, we were both in the massacre at the gay nightclub and, for some reason, we got back together.

JOSE E: Maybe the fear of terror.

MUNA: I've heard that. It's possible. Terror kept us together. But when I think that's what's bringing us together, I want to run and leave everything behind, including her. But when I come to these meetings all I think about is getting home, shutting the door, turning off the TV and holding her until I fall asleep beside her. Safe and asleep. The sleep of freedom.

JOSE E: How many people died at the nightclub?

MUNA: Thirteen.

JOSE E: How many at the restaurant?

SOPHIE: Four dead cops.

JOSE E: Two hundred in the federal building.

SOPHIE: Unbelievable!

MUNA: It's so barbaric!

JOSE E: Absolute brutality, pure brutality.

SOPHIE: Did you see the truck that plowed into that crowd? Horrific. I'm embarrassed to say it but the truth is every time I see that breaking news box flash onscreen about an attack somewhere, without even thinking I go for my calendar to see what I've got coming up. Cause it's practically a given they'll call me for a show.

MUNA: That's awful!

SOPHIE: Yeah, but apparently there's no one like me for talking tragedy.

MUNA: It's hard for me to come to these encounters. I'd rather not relive them. But they keep insisting. They say I can help, that since I'm from Lebanon I have a special point of view. A Muslim, they say, is what we need. And it sounds like they're talking about a quota they need for the show. But I'm not a believer, I don't even pray, and the last time I went to a mosque was as a tourist. I saw it from a distance and I didn't even like it. It scared me. In any case they didn't let me in.

JOSE E: They didn't? Because you're a woman?

MUNA: A woman and gay, you'll say next.

SOPHIE: Then say no.

MUNA: I feel bad doing that; I figure they'll take it as a slight. Call it ethnic guilt. I come from a Muslim country and I can't help feeling condemned and I say yes to everything. At first the shows were really beautiful: people were sympathetic, they supported you, they kept saying how they didn't blame me and all. But in the end they just want to argue and insult people.

SOPHIE: You defend your ideas; speak up, interrupt anyone who contradicts what you think, be fiery and if you need to, insult them. Even if you don't feel it, act like you do. Practice in the mirror. Go on the offensive. You're the victim and you have the right to do whatever you please on camera. The whole world will understand you and they'll take your side.

JOSE E: So how do you do it?

SOPHIE: One day I told myself: from now on I'm going to be belligerent and fight everyone on everything.

JOSE E: You decided that after the attack?

SOPHIE: Long before that, I was a girl practically. I was a normal teenager, a bit chubby, too tall for my age, with a kinda squarish head that made me look funny. The truth is I wasn't like the other pretty girls at school. And I was quiet too, shy really. Back then, everyone bullied me. They teased me, hid my stuff. One time at school they took my desk apart and put it together with wires so when I sat down it'd fall to pieces. And that's just what happened and everyone laughed.

MUNA: And then?

SOPHIE: Then, one day when I got home from school, I decided to be someone else.

MUNA: Just like that?

SOPHIE: Just like that.

MUNA: I'm envious!

JOSE E: Someone else how?

SOPHIE: I decided to be bad. (*MUNA looks at her in surprise. JOSE looks to MUNA for an explanation.*) Not bad bad, but I started doing bad stuff to other people, to kids who were smaller than me. That's when I realized that nearly all of them were weaker or smaller or stranger, weirder than me.

MUNA: What would you do to them?

SOPHIE: Oh, leave dead animals in their lockers or superglue their locks or yank their hair till hanks of it came out in my hand. I had this book where I collected the hanks of my classmates' hair; boys, girls, everyone. I wouldn't let them talk, I'd interrupt, I'd yell, I'd raise my voice even to ask for permission or say sorry.
And that's when they stopped bullying me.
For me, those were the best days of my life. I even lost weight and my head quit being square!

JOSE E: I don't want to hurt anyone…

SOPHIE: That's what white men in this country have come to. Surrender. Or submission more like.

MUNA: (*Pointing to JOSE*) But he's not white…

SOPHIE: What?

JOSE E: Please…

MUNA: He's Latino.

SOPHIE: Latino? But… Really?

JOSE E: That doesn't matter.

SOPHIE: *(Harassing him)* Why do you dress like that, Joe?

JOSE E: Like what?

SOPHIE: I don't know, like a white white guy.

JOSE E: *(Looking at his skin)* I am white white.

SOPHIE: You know what I mean. Is your name Joe Spine?

JOSE E: It's the name I use now to…

SOPHIE: So what's your real name?

JOSE E: In this country you have the right to take the name you want.

SOPHIE: What's your name? Jose? Joe for Jose?

JOSE E: That's what I like about the United States: you can be reborn as many times as you want.

SOPHIE: Spine? *(Laughs. Her mockery is harassment.)* Spine like what? Like a porcupine? *(MUNA and JOSE look at her in shock.)* Pardon me, I don't mean to insult you, but to me it's funny. *(To MUNA)* Don't you think it's funny wanting to be a different race?

MUNA: *(Terrified)* No. I don't know. It's just I don't understand.

JOSE E: I'm Spine for Espinoza.

SOPHIE: And you're from…?

JOSE E: El Salvador.

SOPHIE: Of course you are!

JOSE E: What do you mean "of course you are?"

SOPHIE: That if you take a good look at you, setting aside your clothes, your haircut and your face, of course you come from El Salvador.

JOSE E: Not from Guatemala? Or Costa Rica?

SOPHIE: I don't know anyone from Costa Rica.

JOSE E: But you do from El Salvador.

SOPHIE: Yes, a lot. We had a janitor at the school from there.

JOSE E: Yeah, Jose Espinoza…

SOPHIE: No, his name was… *(Looks at him carefully. She's surprised.)* Jose? Is that you? *(JOSE nods. SOPHIE's attitude changes immediately. Suddenly, she's more herself, more friendly.)* I'm sorry, I didn't recognize you! You've changed so much! *(To MUNA)* We used to work together at the school! He was… !

JOSE E: The janitor.

SOPHIE: I didn't recognize you with…

JOSE E: Without my coveralls.

SOPHIE: Why'd you change the way you look? You're not running from something?

(MUNA, nervous, edges away a little.)

SOPHIE: Jose, I know what I said isn't... I mean, I want you to know that I'm not racist. *(JOSE doesn't answer.)* Also, you have to understand it's not normal to all of a sudden see someone you know and they look like someone else. Can you imagine if I dressed up as a Hispanic woman, with a fruity hat, or an Arab woman covered head to toe? It could be offensive. *(To MUNA)* Right?

(MUNA nervous, feels forced to nod.)

JOSE E: I have to do it. I have to look like someone else. Joe Spine is better than Jake Black and, definitely, ten million times better than Jose Espinoza.

SOPHIE: You committed a crime and now you're in disguise? Is that it?

JOSE E: A crime? Because I come from El Salvador?

SOPHIE: It's not out of the question, is it?

JOSE E: Because I look like a gang member, a raper of white women, because I take jobs from good people like you.

SOPHIE: I mean if you're running from someone.

JOSE E: Of course I am. Where do you think we are?

SOPHIE: You sure you're not hiding something, Jose? A week ago I met this Mexican bigamist, or cuadrigamist, 'cause he'd married four women. And all of them blondes.

MUNA: *(Trying to defend him, but weak and nervous)* I don't think Jose thinks that way...

SOPHIE: *(To MUNA)* Men are men, sugar. Though I guess you aren't really an expert on that, are you?

(MUNA, hurt, turns and walks away.)

JOSE E: Tell me something: is it a requirement?

SOPHIE: What?

JOSE E: Insulting people. Is it really necessary?

SOPHIE: Me? I never insult anyone. I'm 100% open and I accept all kinds.

JOSE E: A little respect wouldn't hurt. A little, not much, a pinch, a whiff, of respect. It doesn't cost you anything, not even an effort. Fake it if you have to. But respect. Don't you think?

SOPHIE: I... *(Sorry, she surprises MUNA)* Miss, Sayeh? Muna? What a pretty name. Muna, I'm sorry. Really. Sometimes I'm a bit impulsive and I don't think before I speak. If you're gay or Muslim, whatever. I don't care, you know. There's no reason for me to care.

(MUNA, suddenly leans against one of the tables, weak.)

MUNA: I...

SOPHIE: And it's true: just because you're from there, from the Muslims or Arabs, doesn't make you a terrorist. I know that, I never doubted that.

JOSE E: *(Keeping SOPHIE from saying something worse)* But you never said anything like that!

SOPHIE: *(To JOSE)* But I might've thought it. *(To MUNA)* Just in case, I'm sorry. And we have something in common: you said you're not religious. I don't think I am either, though I believe in God. How about you?

MUNA: *(Trying to hold herself up)* No, I don't believe in God.

SOPHIE: What do you believe in then?

MUNA: In life...

SOPHIE: Simple. I like that. Me too. We should start a new religion; people who believe in life. Period. (Goes over to her) You see? We're not so different.

(But MUNA is about to faint. SOPHIE manages to catch her before she falls.)

SOPHIE: *(To JOSE)* Quick, bring me that cushion!

(SOPHIE eases her down into a seat.)

JOSE E: *(Getting the cushion)* What's wrong with her?

SOPHIE: I think her blood sugar dropped or something. *(Places the cushion to support her head in the chair.)* Should we call 911?

MUNA: No, it's nothing. I'm fine now. It'll pass.

SOPHIE: Have you eaten today?

MUNA: Yes, of course. It's not that.

SOPHIE: You couldn't be pregnant?

(MUNA laughs.)

MUNA: If I am, then I'll start believing in God. In all of them at once.

(JOSE comes with some water.)

SOPHIE: (*Friendly*) Well, but the night is dark and you never know where the fish will jump.

JOSE E: What fish?

(The two women laugh. MUNA drinks.)

SOPHIE: *(To MUNA)* Better?

JOSE E: The best thing for you is to go home.

MUNA: I'm fine now. It passes over quickly. It's happened before, it's nothing to worry about.

JOSE E: What is it?

MUNA: It happens when I get really nervous.

SOPHIE: Why are you nervous? Cause of what I said? Look, just between you and me and don't tell anyone I said this, but I'm saying it anyhow: you shouldn't pay any attention to me. Okay?

MUNA: It's not you. It's fights, arguments...

JOSE E: Arguments? If someone raises their voice, if you think there could be a fight?

MUNA: That's it. But it doesn't last. My girlfriend says it's because I'm gay and Lebanese.

SOPHIE: *(Trying to be funny)* Well no wonder! *(Sees her joke doesn't go over well.)* It's a joke!

JOSE E: *(To MUNA)* Is it always dizziness?

MUNA: Or aches in my muscles and bones. Sometimes I need help changing my clothes.

SOPHIE: Now that sounds sexy. No one helps me put on clothes, much less take them off.

MUNA: *(Laughs)* In my case, it hurts so much someone has to help me.

SOPHIE: They didn't prescribe Oxy, by any chance? When the lightning got me, those little pills were a godsend.

JOSE E: So what else happens, besides the pain?

MUNA: Sometimes I feel like I don't exist and I have to ask myself: Am I here or not here? I disappear and reappear.

SOPHIE: Now that's too much. I'm sure it's post traumatic stress from the attack.

MUNA: Did you have it?

SOPHIE: After the shooting at the restaurant, of course I did. But after a while it went away.

MUNA: How?

SOPHIE: First, anti-anxiety meds. Then, Gatorade. Huge bottles of Gatorade three times a day. Though lately I quit all that cause, to be honest, the only thing that works for me is alcohol.

JOSE E: *(To MUNA)* Just out of curiosity; do you forget things all the time?

MUNA: *(Surprised)* Yes! All the everyday stuff.

JOSE E: And do you feel like you could shatter any second?

MUNA: That's it! I walk down the street and I think the breeze will break me. If I stumble on a rock I'll break my foot, if someone shakes my hand they'll break my fingers.

JOSE E: It's classic.

MUNA: You know what it is?

SOPHIE: Really?

JOSE E: What you have is known as the Glass Delusion.

(The two women look at him skeptically.)

SOPHIE: How do you know?

MUNA: Glass?

JOSE E: People who think they're made of glass and liable to shatter.

MUNA: A delusion? Like I'm crazy?

JOSE E: It's not crazy, no one's crazy. Maybe the people who want to hurt people are the crazies. But a sick person is sick, not crazy.

SOPHIE: How do you know about this glass thing?

JOSE E: The same way I know everything I know: reading.

SOPHIE: Reading, just like that.

JOSE E: The thing is in El Salvador I was a Geography professor.

MUNA: *(Almost laughing)* And what's Geography got to do with glass?

SOPHIE: A professor? And you came here to be a plain old workman?

JOSE E: That's why I got a job in the school. To remember what it's like to be surrounded by students and devote myself to them. Even if it's as a janitor and not in front of a classroom.

SOPHIE: So how does a Geography professor know about medical stuff?

JOSE E: Like the Glass Delusion?

SOPHIE: Yeah, that Delusion thing.

JOSE E: The Glass Delusion is well documented. Today it's known as a syndrome, there's medication and treatment, but at one time it was considered a type of madness. Cervantes has a character with that syndrome.

SOPHIE: Who?

JOSE E: Cervantes. You know, Don Quixote?

SOPHIE: Don Corleone? Don Corleone pizzas?

JOSE E: That's the one. He's got loads of pizzas for gangsters.

SOPHIE: I haven't tried them.

JOSE E: He has a story about the Glass Graduate, who thinks his body is made of glass and that at any time it will shatter.

MUNA: That's me. That's how I am.

JOSE E: Me too. Me too.

MUNA: You believe you're made of glass too?

JOSE E: No, but I believe that if I'm not someone else, I'll be erased. Black, white, Asian. Anything but what I am. So I won't disappear.

MUNA: I guess that's an illness too.

JOSE E: Miss Muna, the thing is your glass delusion and my desire to become someone else, are a way of handling humiliation.

(Someone knocks on the door. The three look at the door, expectantly, with some terror. Then the school intercom comes on.)

VOICE: Your attention please: the Sensibility Class encounter will begin in a few minutes. All interested students, please head to the auditorium. With us today are Muna Sayeh, Sophie Glenn and Joe Spin. I mean, Joe Spine. Sorry. Welcome to our school!

SOPHIE *(Taking charge of everything)* Okay y'all. Unless they say otherwise, it'll probably go like this: They'll ask: who wants to speak first? I'll go. Ok? For fifteen minutes or so. My story, the lightning strikes, the attack, etc. Then, I won't say anything else till the question and answer session. Oh! And don't get upset if

I interrupt you at some point. It's just hard for me to keep quiet. All right?

MUNA: Yeah, sure. My part will be quick.

JOSE E: They'll hardly see me. *(To MUNA)* How do you feel?

MUNA: Much better.

SOPHIE: Good. *(Trying to joke)* And don't forget, no shattering in front of the students.

MUNA: Of course. After all, that's why we're here.

SOPHIE: *(Laughs)* That's right. And you should be happy.

MUNA: Why?

SOPHIE: They said your name first.

MUNA: What?

SOPHIE: When they announced us, they said your name first.

MUNA: That doesn't matter to me.

SOPHIE: Really? Do you mind if I ask them to change the order?

MUNA: Not at all!

SOPHIE Fine. Let's go then.

(SOPHIE initiates a group hug. The others go along. The hug is intense. SOPHIE opens the door and JOSE goes out first. When MUNA is heading out past

SOPHIE, SOPHIE stops her. MUNA is a bit frightened. SOPHIE looks at her as if searching for the words she needs to say but can't find them.)

SOPHIE: (*After a pause and with a sincerity we haven't seen in the rest of the play*) You know what? All that about the delusion. I… I think I'm like you.

MUNA: You mean…?

SOPHIE: That I have the Glass Delusion too. I just get the feeling that I'm about to shatter any second.

MUNA: You?

SOPHIE: Yes, me. That's it. (*Certain*) I have the Glass Delusion. But with lightning. Glass shattered by a lightning bolt.

(*MUNA laughs and hugs her. Suddenly, she gives her a peck on the lips.*)

MUNA: You're the best of the bad.

(*They laugh more, like they'd gotten up to something and go out holding hands. Music.*)

2/ DR. BIRDEN'S OFFICE

(Waiting room. Chairs, paintings and a door that leads to a room labeled "Interviews." Onstage, ROBERT, in his uniform. With him, SELENA and MCKEEMAN. All three wear a sticker on their chest with their last name followed by a smiley face.)

ROBERT: The stadium?

SELENA: No, not that one.

ROBERT: I was at the highway one, the religious commune one and the shooting at the beach. Oh! And the airport one too.

SELENA: That one! The airport one! I remember it! The time the experts didn't let us talk. I think I said one thing and you didn't say anything. Right?

ROBERT: Nothing, they hardly put me on.

SELENA: *(To MCKEEMAN)* What about you?

MCKEEMAN: *(Sullen)* I haven't been to anything.

SELENA: Didn't they invite you? Because you're so young and…

MCKEEMAN: I don't care.

SELENA: Yours was at….?

MCKEEMAN: You need to stop talking to me, "sista."

SELENA: I just wanted to…

MCKEEMAN: Yeah I know. Leave me alone if you don't want trouble.

ROBERT: Hey! Some respect, kid.

MCKEEMAN: Then both of you leave me alone. And my name's not kid. That's all.

ROBERT: She was only asking to make conversation, but believe me neither of us is interested in you at all, or your story.

MCKEEMAN: Good.

ROBERT: You're young, but that's nothing to brag about, kid.

MCKEEMAN: Whatever. But I'm here because it's a requirement, so I'm not quite in the same mood as the two of you. And don't call me kid!

SELENA: A requirement? You're here by court order?

(A gesture from the boy confirms SELENA's suspicion.)

ROBERT: No wonder he's got a bug up his butt.

SELENA: I don't agree with those orders. *(Reading the name on his chest)* McKeeman? McKeeman. Right. I'm Selena. *(She's going to shake his hand but sees it's pointless.)* So, I was saying, McKeeman, those orders don't accomplish anything. Actually, they do the opposite: the kids get more violent.

MCKEEMAN: *(Violent)* I'm not violent!

ROBERT: *(Threatening)* Calm down or I'll calm you down!

MCKEEMAN: With your fists.

ROBERT: You give the impression you could use it.

SELENA: Ignore him, officer. He's a teenager. We were all that way.

ROBERT: I never had the luxury.

SELENA: We all did.

ROBERT: Not me. My father wouldn't let me raise my voice. (*Shows his shoulder*) Look…

SELENA: What is that?

ROBERT: When I was more or less the same age as this delinquent *(Pointing to MCKEEMAN)*, I raised my voice to my mother. And my dad, without stopping to think twice, threw a chair at me. The chair broke and this huge nail stuck me like a knife.

SELENA: And what did they do to your father?

ROBERT: They didn't need to do anything to him because he was teaching me a lesson, that's what his partners said. And they were right. I never raised my voice at home again.

SELENA: His partners? You father was a police officer too?

ROBERT: Third generation in blue. And to give the story a happy ending, I'll tell you my father had a scar almost just like this on his back.

MCKEEMAN: (*Suddenly, loud*) All this bullshit talking makes me want to puke! When is this shit…? *(ROBERT shoots him a menacing look. MCKEEMAN lowers his voice.)* What a long and interesting conversation here in the reception area. Now, my question is: when is the interview going to start? If I may be so bold and if it's no bother, could one of the adults present please be so kind as to inform me.

(SELENA laughs. ROBERT leans back from him, satisfied.)

SELENA: Dr. Birden called to say he'd be a little late. Traffic, he said.

ROBERT: Now that's strange. These sessions always start on time.

SELENA: Do you do a lot of them?

ROBERT: Most of them voluntarily, others because they pay and some, sure, by court order. They're good. At least you relax; you remember but you forget too. I enjoy them, just not so close together or I get bored. But they told me this one's new. What's it called?

SELENA: Consultation on Radicalization.

ROBERT: Right. That word, Radicalization. What's it got to do with us?

MCKEEMAN: Right! What the fuck does that shit have to do with me? (*Lowers his voice*) What possible relation can there be between this encounter and yours truly?

SELENA: The idea is to talk to Dr. Birden, who's an expert on Radicalization, to give him all the information we can on what happened to us. Or what we witnessed. No one's accusing us of being radicals, of course. He just wants to know what we think. He's looking for patterns so he can identify the context that people who become radicalized are living in.

ROBERT: You'll have to excuse me, because you sound like an intelligent and cultured person, but that seems silly. Where do radicals come from? From religion, from poverty, from race and all that. From a lack of family values, of patriotism and a mother and father who know how to teach…

MCKEEMAN: With a chair to the head, for instance.

ROBERT: Right. Because a chair to the head at the right moment stops you, instead of turning radical and going off and killing people, you want to be a cop and help others. You see? A well-timed chair to the head. You want one McKeeman?

MCKEEMAN: No, thanks.

ROBERT: (*Again, to SELENA*) This country's gone to hell, it's lost. That's the context: a lack of country. What they should do is look for the radicals and ask them. But, us? We're not radicals. Though the kid, are you or aren't you?

MCKEEMAN: Don't call me kid!

ROBERT: Are you a radical or not, kid?

MCKEEMAN: (*Restrains himself*) I'm nothing.

ROBERT: That's what I was saying, you act like nothing, you look like nothing and you talk like nothing. Nothing, no doubt about it; you're a radical/Nothing.

(*MCKEEMAN's going to answer back but ROBERT's look intimidates him.*)

MCKEEMAN: Whatever you say, captain.

ROBERT: Sargent's more like it.

MCKEEMAN: *(Sarcastic)* With the uniform who could tell.

ROBERT: A cop isn't a uniform. The cop is inside you.

MCKEEMAN: You've got a cop inside you? You like him inside you?

(ROBERT is annoyed but SELENA stops him.)

SELENA: Did the two of you read the material they gave us when we got here? It talks precisely about language as radicalization, as violence. As context. You understand?

ROBERT: Of course, it's just kids like him are the ones who turn you so radical that suddenly all you want to do is break their face, in context, of course.

MCKEEMAN: Yeah, particularly in the context of killing cops, right?

ROBERT: Is that it? You want to kill me, kid?

MCKEEMAN: Don't call me kid!

ROBERT: You hate me? Is it just me you want to kill or someone else too? The young lady here? Her too?

MCKEEMAN: No, not her.

ROBERT: And you have a list, right?

MCKEEMAN: Of course. We all have a list of the people we want to kill.

ROBERT: So who's on it?

MCKEEMAN: Just pigs like you and filthy Muslims. It'll be a mass but sweeping execution: against all of them.

SELENA: The ones at the concert, they were jihadists, right?

MCKEEMAN: Goddamn Arabs.

SELENA: Arabs? Sunnis, Shiites?

MCKEEMAN: What?

SELENA: Did they speak Arabic, Urdu or Farsi?

MCKEEMAN: Huh?

SELENA: Were they from outside or were they homegrown in the United States of America?

MCKEEMAN: They were all shit!

ROBERT: I agree with you there. Pure shit.

SELENA: Tell me, McKeeman, what do you remember about the men who shot you?

MCKEEMAN: That they were shit.

SELENA: Aside from that, I'm sure they were. They attacked a concert by the…What were they called?

MCKEEMAN: Zombie Harpies!

SELENA: Right. What were they like?

MCKEEMAN: The bassist was the best in the world and the drummer too…

SELENA: I mean the men who shot you.

MCKEEMAN: Shitty terroris-

SELENA: Of course. Shitty. But…what do you remember about them?

MCKEEMAN: Nothing. Nothing…

SELENA: Tell us…

MCKEEMAN: I, I don't know.

SELENA: It was in the middle of the concert, wasn't it? I heard during the break.

MCKEEMAN: It was at the beginning. In the middle of a song.

ROBERT: What animals!

MCKEEMAN: *(Agitated)* Yeah, animals! Exactly! Shitty brutal animals!

SELENA: The music was playing and then…

MCKEEMAN: In the middle of the music, and everyone happy, planning their future, those animals whipped out machine guns and started spraying bullets. At everyone, they didn't care about race, nationality, age, nothing. Just shooting!

SELENA: Why do you think they did it?

MCKEEMAN: Because they hate us! Foreigners hate us!

SELENA: But the terrorists were from here.

MCKEEMAN: No, they weren't from here!

SELENA: They were born in this country. Went to school here. Watched the same TV shows you did, that we all did.

MCKEEMAN: But they hate me! They've always hated me!

SELENA: You?

MCKEEMAN: And I hate them too! It's mutual!

SELENA: But, why do you say they hated you, in particular?

ROBERT: Did they know you?

MCKEEMAN: They hated me!

SELENA: You?

MCKEEMAN: *(Angry, in climax)* Yes, me, me, me, me, me, me, me, me!

ROBERT: Why you?

MCKEEMAN: Because they killed Katie!

(SELENA and ROBERT are shocked.)

SELENA: Katie?

(MCKEEMAN paces back and forth. He checks that no one else is listening.)

MCKEEMAN: I was on one knee, asking Katie to marry me, like the man from the future said I should. So she'd be my partner and we could start the resistance against the domination by... others. I don't remember who... Blacks? Foreigners? Something like that. I don't remember now. The man from the future told me he'd come to let me know how important I was and that my name would be famous and there'd be streets and airports named after me in his time, in 2216. And Katie, Katie too, she'd be known as a fighter who freed her people. She'd be my muse, my inspiration, my only love. And when I was proposing to her to start the future once and for all, then, she got shot. She said a few words and died in my arms.

SELENA: What about you? What did you do?

MCKEEMAN: That's all I saw. I had a Glock in my jacket, this same one, but I didn't do anything. I didn't defend her. I didn't avenge myself.

SELENA: You were wearing that same jacket?

MCKEEMAN: No, this same Glock.

(MCKEEMAN, like nothing, pulls out the Glock. He holds it by the butt without touching the trigger, like someone dangling a bouquet of flowers upside down. ROBERT is alarmed by the gun and SELENA moves away, but not far. She covers her mouth.)

ROBERT: What are you doing with that?

MCKEEMAN: Nick, the guy who said he came from the future warned me this was going to happen...

ROBERT: Give it to me. You should give it to me...

MCKEEMAN: And now that I think about it, he probably wasn't from the future or anything...

ROBERT: (*Moving closer*) We're really sorry, but the best thing you can do is give me that...

MCKEEMAN: He just wanted to get rid of me...

ROBERT: *(Closer. MCKEEMAN keeps the gun toward the floor.)* I got you...I got you, but that could start trouble...

MCKEEMAN: And stay in my house for free and also screw my mom, for free too.

(*MCKEEMAN hands ROBERT the gun very calmly and turns away from them, hiding his face. ROBERT puts the gun away.*)

ROBERT: *(To SELENA)* I better hold on to this. I'll take it to headquarters tomorrow.

SELENA: Don't get him in any more trouble.

ROBERT: If the gun's clean, of course not.

(SELENA sees MCKEEMAN has shrunk, hiding his face. Maybe he's crying. She goes to hug him but then MCKEEMAN reacts violently. He pushes her and moves away. SELENA loses her balance a bit, but recovers quickly. ROBERT grabs a chair, like he's going to hit MCKEEMAN, but SELENA stops him.)

SELENA: (*To ROBERT*) Don't pay attention to him.

ROBERT: I'm not paying attention to him, of course not. *(He sets the chair aside and sits in it, justifying his earlier action with humor. MCKEEMAN throws himself to the ground and hides in his jacket.)*

SELENA: At his age, you fill the space of what you don't understand with violence.

ROBERT: It's no wonder. I guess all three of us have that empty space, don't we?

SELENA: I know I do.

ROBERT: Me too. Do you work here with Dr. Birden?

SELENA: No, I'm an immigration lawyer. But since I was a victim of an attack, here I am.

ROBERT: A victim of which attack?

SELENA: Of two attacks, actually!

MCKEEMAN: *(Coming out of hiding)* Two! That fucking sucks! *(Looks to ROBERT)* Oh good heavens! Oh, how cruel!

ROBERT: What luck! If you don't mind, what attacks were you in?

MCKEEMAN: *(Excited)* At the concert? Were you at the Zombie Harpies concert? Did you see when they shot us?

SELENA: No, I wasn't at the concert. But I was in the massacre at the gay bar and then in the federal building.

MCKEEMAN: GAY! *(MCKEEMAN laughs idiotically. ROBERT looks at him and then mechanically he stops laughing.)* Fluid…uh…gender…uh…I don't know.

ROBERT: And you escaped both of them. *(Reading her name tag)* Mrs. Reynolds. Wow.

SELENA: Miss Reynolds.

ROBERT: You being a lawyer and all.

SELENA: *(Fed up)* Yeah, yeah, yeah. Call me Selena.

ROBERT: The impressive thing is being able to say you, whether you're a miss or a missus or a cop, managed to escape two terrorist attacks.

SELENA: But same as McKeeman and same as you, the truth is there's no escape.

ROBERT: No, of course not. I mean you got out of both still breathing.

SELENA: Breathing underwater. That's why I volunteer for every study on the subject. I want to help but I want to know. Like him *(Pointing to MCKEEMAN)* filling my empty spaces.

MCKEEMAN: Know what? That there are evil people killing us?

SELENA: I want to know what's underneath all this.

ROBERT: Well, good for you, Selena. But for me, empty or full, this ends today.

SELENA: What do you mean?

ROBERT: I'm withdrawing. I don't want to answer any more questions. Today's session with Dr. Birden on radicalization, is my last.

SELENA: Think it over, Robert. You still have a lot to contribute. A police officer has a unique perspective. Also, you survived a racist attack.

ROBERT: You said it: truly racist. The bastard wanted to kill white cops! No gray areas. Just white ones. Though one of the victims was a black officer...

SELENA: African-American.

ROBERT: I guess the killer didn't see very well.

SELENA: You see? You have a lot to say...

ROBERT: But there's no going back, Miss. I'm withdrawing. *(SELENA is going to keep trying but he interrupts her)* My answers are always the same; I don't have anything new to say. My son Alex has recorded my TV interviews and when he puts them on, I feel so ashamed. I feel stupid. Like I was saying what happened without understanding it, without the words you need to say so you don't sound like an idiot.

SELENA: How old is your son?

ROBERT: *(Looking at MCKEEMAN)* He's a teenager now. Fifteen.

SELENA: Keep trying a little longer. Pick a date: a year or six months more. Then, make your decision.

ROBERT: *(In a serious tone)* I don't know. Because there's the reporters too.

SELENA: What's going on with them?

ROBERT: You don't know?

SELENA: What?

ROBERT: My history. My past. You don't know? It was big news...

SELENA: What happened?

ROBERT: I figured you had recognized me.

SELENA: Is there something else, besides the shooting in the restaurant with the police?

ROBERT: Yes, of course. Though everything, like you say, is context.

SELENA: What things about your past?

ROBERT: The usual. The things that happen in the life of a cop.

SELENA: Like for example?

ROBERT: Like for example before the attack at the restaurant I was suspended over baseless accusations.

SELENA: What accusations?

ROBERT: It was an accident, of course…

SELENA: Of course it was. But, what did they accuse you of?

MCKEEMAN: Police brutality.

ROBERT: Stay out of it!

SELENA: Brutality? Here? In this city? *(Stares at him and remembers.)* Of course, I saw it on the news! Of course! There was an uproar in our community. My brothers went to the protests… You!

ROBERT: Don't believe everything you heard at the time. I swear it was an accident. Believe me.

SELENA: You shot an African-American driving on 95. Robert, why?

ROBERT: It was an accident, a mistake.

SELENA: But, how did it happen?

ROBERT: I've talked too much about this...

SELENA: Please, it's a golden opportunity. To understand you.

ROBERT: That won't be possible, miss.

SELENA: There are no cameras here. It's just us. You can be honest.

ROBERT: Like I said, it was an accident. An accident.

(Pause. He stands and moves away a little.)

SELENA: Yes?

ROBERT: That afternoon we were looking for a robbery suspect, a black man...

SELENA: African-American

ROBERT: African-American. A robbery at a store. We had a description and even a photo on the computer from the security camera. When I was driving down 95 I saw a car and a driver who looked a lot like, almost identical to the suspect.

SELENA: Almost identical?

ROBERT: The same features...as...You know...

MCKEEMAN: A black dude.

SELENA: As an African-American?

ROBERT: Right. The braids, his features, his heavy build, the big nose.

(MCKEEMAN laughs.)

SELENA: The big nose?

ROBERT: Yes, like the suspect.

SELENA: I have a big nose!

(MCKEEMAN laughs.)

ROBERT: I don't mean you.

SELENA: I'm black! It's my race!

ROBERT: Yes, but...

SELENA: Isn't it the same?

ROBERT: It's not the same.

MCKEEMAN: It's not the same!

(MCKEEMAN laughs. ROBERT takes a chair, no violence to the gesture, and looks at MCKEEMAN.)

ROBERT: Behave or I'll sit you in the corner.

(MCKEEMAN stops laughing.)

SELENA: Robert, then?

ROBERT: Then I pulled him over. I asked the suspect for his ID and when he went to get his papers from the glove compartment, I saw he had a gun there. I thought he'd use it against me and somehow, I shot him.

SELENA: You thought he was going to pull out the gun?

ROBERT: I thought he came from a robbery!

SELENA: But it wasn't him!

ROBERT: No, it wasn't him.

SELENA: And he had a gun?

ROBERT: Yes, a legally owned gun.

SELENA: What was he doing with a gun?

ROBERT: He didn't have to be doing anything. He had one, that's all.

SELENA: For protection?

ROBERT: That's what his family said. But I thought he was going to shoot me.

SELENA: Just like with McKeeman.

ROBERT: No, not like with him.

SELENA: He had a gun.

ROBERT: But it was obvious that…

SELENA: And he had it in his hand, not the glove compartment of his car.

ROBERT: But…

SELENA: And with him you didn't think he was going to shoot you, but with the other guy you did?

ROBERT: Selena, they're two different situations. You saw when this kid took out the gun but he didn't really try anything...

SELENA: "Really" I don't know. Why?

ROBERT: Because he...

SELENA: Because he's white?

ROBERT: That's not important...

SELENA: He's white and he looks like your fifteen-year-old son Alex?

ROBERT: *(Looks at her like he's been stabbed in the back.)* No. No. It's not...It's not that. What I'm trying to say is the other case was an accident. *(He continues looking at SELENA, who stares him down. ROBERT gives in.)* Don't judge me, Miss, everyone's done that already...

SELENA: I'm not judging you. I'm not. *(She realizes that she is judging him.)* I'm sorry. I didn't mean to. *(Beat)* So what did they do about it?

ROBERT: Well, nothing. His family buried him and there was...

SELENA: I mean to you.

ROBERT: After the accident they suspended me.

SELENA: But you're in uniform.

ROBERT: After the restaurant attack they reinstated me.

SELENA: And you're armed?

ROBERT: Well, now I am.

(ROBERT thinks SELENA is going to explode, but instead she approaches him supportively.)

SELENA: You see? You see how important your perspective is?

ROBERT: *(Confused)* What? On what? On this?

SELENA: Of course, on this.

ROBERT: I don't think it's relevant.

SELENA: Yes, of course it is.

ROBERT: What the hell does what I did have to do with radicalization? Isn't this about Arabs?

SELENA: It's relevant: your son, your gun, your opinions.

ROBERT: I don't see the relation.

SELENA: It's known as a Frame of Reference and it has to do with what's invisible.

MCKEEMAN: *(Repeating what SELENA says, considering)* It has to do with what's invisible…

ROBERT: Are you mocking me?

SELENA: Prejudice comes from the way we define ourselves. It's invisible because it's made up of things we can't see. Emotions, comparisons, competition, but also language, insults, offensiveness.

MCKEEMAN: Yeah, but the guys who killed Katie weren't invisible.

(MCKEEMAN turns around and moves away from them, as though deciding to leave the conversation.)

SELENA: *(To MCKEEMAN)* Of course not. But there are other things that are. *(To ROBERT)* Listen, Robert, I'm not going to bother you any more. I'm sure we'll have a chance to talk about this in the consultation. But since they're private interviews, I'm curious...

ROBERT: Of course you are.

SELENA: Can I ask you a question?

ROBERT: Can I avoid it?

SELENA: I swear it'll be the last one.

ROBERT: Fine. Shoot.

SELENA: What?

ROBERT: Ask your question.

SELENA: The black man who was driving his car on 95...

ROBERT: African-American.

SELENA: Exactly him...

ROBERT: Yes?

SELENA: Couldn't you see him as a person just like you?

ROBERT: What?

SELENA: Like a while ago with McKeeman. It was obvious for a second you saw him like he was your son. And that had an effect, so a situation that might have ended in violence was resolved like a family matter.

ROBERT: You think so?

SELENA: *(She nods)* So, the African-American man: Didn't you see him as man like you?

(MCKEEMAN turns to hear ROBERT's answer. The police officer, nervous, moves away from SELENA a little.)

ROBERT: I'll be honest. No. I didn't see him as someone like me. Not because he wasn't, maybe he was. I'm sure he was. When I found out he was a teacher, that he'd never had any trouble with the law, that he kept a gun in his glove compartment because he worked in one of the most dangerous parts of the city, parts where no one wants to go, where not even us cops patrol, that's when I realized, yes: that man wasn't so different from me. But at the time of the accident, when I saw he was nervous, when I saw his gun, his features, the way he was looking back at me, like suspicious, like accusing me, then I couldn't.
(Pause. They look at him.)
And I can't.
I can't.
I can't see him as one of my own.
Can't see him or love him as one of my own.
I can't understand them, you know?
Not even you, a good person, who I've been getting to know all this time, I can't.
With him, I can. Looking at him, I thought of my Alex. And I felt upset, I wanted to help him, keep him from ruining his life.

But with the other I can't.
I try, but I can't!
(*Loud*) And the worst part, the reason I haven't been able to sleep since that night, is that I don't know why I can't, Selena!
I don't know! But I swear I can't!
(*Louder. Grabs the chair, like he's going to hit himself in the same place he was hurt before.*)
And I'm sick of it, that I can't!
That I can't and I don't know why terrifies me!
That's it! That's my terrorism!
(*Pause. He looks at MCKEEMAN and puts the chair aside, like setting something very fragile on the floor. Before going on, he gently caresses the chair, as though saying goodbye to it.*)
Though now, a few minutes ago, while I was listening to your story (*Points to MCKEEMAN*) I had a thought.
I had a thought and I remembered something.
And this is it:
That I can't because, for as long as I can remember, <u>they taught me</u> that I shouldn't. That I shouldn't be able to, you understand?
That. They taught me that.
That we're different. That they hate us.
That you have to be afraid of them.
That they carry violence in the color of their skin; violence and failure, that's what they taught me.
Ever since I was a boy that's what I heard my father say at home, to his friends, to my friends, to my mother, to his family, all of them saying the same things over and over that now I say and think too.
You know what? I think that's why I can't. I can't.
(*Beat. There is a very awkward silence. SELENA is going to speak but ROBERT cuts her off.*)
Or I should say, I couldn't.
(*SELENA and MCKEEMAN look at him, incredulous.*)
Because you see now that I know why I can't, then, I think I can. Of course I can!

While I was listening to McKeeman tell his catastrophe I thought he was Alex; his tone of voice, his words, his laugh, like my son's laugh when he's talking to five people at once on the internet. And suddenly, it hit me: Isn't everyone's kid like that?
And now, right this instant, I'm saying to myself:
If that's true, maybe what I have to do is think that their kids are my kids too. Simple as that.
And that's the phrase. I think if I think of it that way, I can.
I can. Don't you think?

SELENA: Robert. In a lot of our families, there's a moment we call "time for the talk." For other people, it's when parents talk to their kids about sex for the first time. "Having the talk," they call it. At twelve or thirteen. But in our homes, besides the sex talk, there's "the other talk." Mom was the one who told me, almost like an order: *(Lightly mimicking her mother)*
Selena, don't forget you're black. You're black. It's not an easy thing to forget, but you might when you're out with your friends, for a second, it might happen. You might forget. Maybe because, for a second, you might think life is freedom. But that feeling will be over fast the first time you have a run-in with the police. Have no doubt: it'll happen to you. I'm not saying you're doing anything wrong; just that, somewhere down the line, you're going to cross paths with the police. And when that happens, don't for any reason forget this moment and the next four things I'm going to tell you:
One: When you speak to that officer, always be respectful and call him "sir."
Two: Make sure the officer can see your hands at all times.
Three: Don't make any sudden movements and anytime you're going to do something, tell him what you're going to do and ask permission first.

And four: It doesn't matter if the officer yells or he's rude, or insults you. No matter what, you ALWAYS behave like you're speaking to your father.
(SELENA goes over to ROBERT finally.)
Then, Robert, I remember I asked: Mom, but why?
And then like it was the simplest thing in the world, she said: *(Lightly mimicking her mother)*
Because that man has the power to kill you.
And we have no power to seek justice.
And both of those things are known and understood on both sides.
(Beat)
That's when Dad spoke up and said the key phrase of the evening. He said: Sweetheart, in the end, it's all about Power.

(ROBERT looks at her, ashamed.)

ROBERT: Selena, I don't...I don't have power.

SELENA: I'm telling you this because those were the words I remembered when the bomb went off in the federal building; when I started asking myself how the two things might be connected; and when the second attack happened at the gay nightclub where I'd spent so many of my happy moments. While they were shooting fear at us, I remembered my parents' words about what an encounter between an African American and a police officer means, or rather, between a helpless person and Power. And listening to you, Robert, I got it. Yes, there is a connection.

ROBERT: And what is it?

SELENA: That indiscriminate brutality arises from indiscriminate contempt.

(Suddenly, there's a knock at the door. We hear a voice.)

VOICE: Sargent Robert Glenn; they're ready for you.

ROBERT: I guess I'm going first. *(Leaving, he shakes SELENA's hand.)* Just in case I don't see you again, let me say it was a pleasure. A pleasure.

SELENA: For me too.

(They shake hands, cordial. ROBERT goes to say goodbye to MCKEEMAN but does it with a youthful gesture from the door.)

ROBERT: Take care, kid. *(Regretful)* Sorry. Ethan. Ethan McKeeman: take care. *(Points to where he put the Glock away)* I'm taking this. *(MCKEEMAN nods, like he doesn't care.)* If you want it back, come find me at the station on Hughey Avenue. Ethan? *(MCKEEMAN nods again.)* And stop spending so much time on the internet!!

(ROBERT said that in the same way he did in Scene One. He chuckles and leaves. MCKEEMAN laughs a bit too, guessing where that came from, and moves away from SELENA a little. She sits down and checks her phone. She makes a call.)

SELENA: Muna, honey? I'm going to be a bit later. Yeah, in Radicalization. But it's going slow; the first one just went in. I guess I'll be next. *(MCKEEMAN gestures like she's completely mistaken.)* Or maybe not. Wait to have dinner with me, ok? And don't watch Game of Thrones without me!!! *(She laughs. Blows kisses and says, in Arabic)* 2حبي و أحبك، أنا

MCKEEMAN: *(Like he'd seen a bomb)* That's Arabic! That's Arabic!

---

[2] *I love you, my darling. / Ana Bahebak Habib Albi*

SELENA: Yeah, my girlfriend is Lebanese. You don't know how hard it's been for me to learn. It's a really hard language!

MCKEEMAN: And what did you say to her?!

SELENA: In Arabic? *(MCKEEMAN nods)* I left her a message. I said, "I love you, my darling." I always want to say that to her, I don't know why. Insecurity maybe. Or just in case something happens and then I'm sorry I didn't say it.

(Then, it happens. MCKEEMAN explodes. It is a horrible pain, a mix of sobbing and gasping. SELENA goes over to him and hugs him.)

MCKEEMAN: Katie...I love you, my darling. Katie...

(SELENA hugs him tighter, like he was a little boy.)

SELENA: She knew. She knew you loved her.

MCKEEMAN: *(Hugging SELENA)* Don't touch me, you're black! Don't touch me! Leave me alone! Leave me alone!

(MCKEEMAN repeats the last dialogue but hugging SELENA like she was his mother. He's interrupted by the VOICE from the door.)

VOICE: Ethan McKeeman, your turn.

(Then, MCKEEMAN feels terrified.)

MCKEEMAN: No, not me. Don't let them see me...

SELENA: Ethan, Ethan, calm down...

MCKEEMAN: I don't know anything. I don't know anything.

SELENA: It's ok. Let it go.

MCKEEMAN: I don't want to go.

SELENA: Do you want me to go first?

MCKEEMAN: No, don't leave me alone.

SELENA: I'm not going to leave you alone.

MCKEEMAN: Tell them we'll come tomorrow.

SELENA: Ok, I'll tell them. Today we're not answering questions.

MCKEEMAN: And we're staying like this.

SELENA: All right,

MCKEEMAN: For a while

SELENA: However long you want

MCKEEMAN: Thanks

(They knock on the door again.)

VOICE: McKeeman?

SELENA: *(Loud)* Leave us alone!

(Music. The lights begin to dim. MCKEEMAN and SELENA alone. Blackout.)

DIVORCE

*"...But it is when all seems safe
and secure for the I,
that the Other bursts in."
Levinas.*

*"The Other is radically Other."
Derrida*

Characters:

TINA GALLOWAY (Female, 40-45) Married, a very popular blogger known for reading and attacking the subtext of what others say.

BEN GALLOWAY (Male, 42-48) Tina's husband. A once successful composer of videogame soundtracks.

Setting:

Master bathroom in the Galloway house. Bathtub at center stage, sink, mirror, glass walled shower and two large windows. The main countertop has dual sinks: one for Tina and the other for Ben. A large walk-in closet with their clothes. To one side, facing the audience, the toilet. Also shelves, a small TV, a wall mounted phone, a large poster with the painting Eleven A.M. by Edward Hopper, and a pendulum clock that reads 11 a.m.

1/ ONE WEEK AGO

(Tina is in the bathtub, lathering up rather sensually. Beside her, a folder of papers and documents, her iPad on top. Ben, in underwear and a dress shirt. He's in the process of getting ready to go out without showering: deodorant, hair gel, quick shave. On the counter several open folders and another iPad playing music. Draped over the glass shower divider, a Superman t-shirt. Elton John's "Tiny Dancer" comes on the iPad. Ben turns up the volume.)

BEN: Your song!

TINA: Turn that off, you idiot.

(Ben sings "Tiny Dancer" and points at Tina dancing in the tub. She pretends she's going to show him a breast. Ben picks up his iPad to take a photo. But when Ben closes in, Tina splashes him. She giggles at her own antics. Ben is annoyed that she got his iPad and shirt wet. He turns off the music and heads to the closet to change his shirt, but first glances out the window. Something catches his eye and he goes closer.)

BEN: The cop's not where he's supposed to be.

TINA: He's probably with the woman across the street.

BEN: Isn't she married?

TINA: Yeah, sure.

BEN: And she's into the cop?

TINA: What's not to be into?

BEN: I don't see the attraction.

TINA: I do.

BEN: Don't beat around the bush.

TINA: I won't, darling. The cop's hot. He takes care of himself. He's got a great body, we can't deny that. None of the neighborhood ladies deny that.

BEN: He's so much younger than you.

TINA: And the woman across the street.

BEN: Her too.

TINA: That doesn't hurt. Are we talking about the tall white cop? Or the black one who looks like a thug? Or the fat elephant?

BEN: I don't know, sweetheart. I can't tell the cops protecting you apart.

TINA: Because that black guy is scary, you know.

BEN: You don't like the African-American guy, you mean.

TINA: The adjective doesn't make him any lighter or darker. And the fat one doesn't get laid even by his own hand. I don't see how that hippo is going to chase down the terrorists when they come. Maybe he'll roll them down.

BEN: You should report him, sweetheart. That the police force in the neighborhood is out seducing wives doesn't make me feel particularly safe.

TINA: I'll report him as long as it's clear that the cute one is the tall white guy.

BEN: I bet the neighbor's husband doesn't think he's so cute.

TINA: What about you?

BEN: Not even a little. Why? Having second thoughts?

TINA: The butt buddy club is a total mystery, you know that.

BEN: I'm serious, Tina.

TINA: So am I. The butt, darling, is... (*Getting out of the tub*) Hand me my towel, si vous play.

(Ben hands it to her. Tina gets out, naked, covered in foam. She wraps the towel around her, holding back laughter)

BEN: It's been a long time since I've seen you undressed.

TINA: What do you think?

BEN: You look great.

TINA: Hate makes me look better. And the gym doesn't hurt, believe me.

(She goes to the window and confirms that there are no police. She makes a fed up gesture.)

BEN: It's not right a cop, sent by the government to protect you, is off merrily seducing the neighbor and neglecting his primary duty.

TINA: Who said he's the one who seduced her?

BEN: Are you saying she jumped him?

TINA: I'm saying it could be the other way around.

BEN: If you're not going take this seriously, I'll drop it. Let 'em pump you full of lead.

TINA: No one's going to pump me full of lead.

BEN: No one?

TINA: Fine: they're all going to pump me full of lead! Even you, if you find someone to do it for you. *(Looks out the window again. Confirms the situation)* It's true. No one's protecting me. Where's the fat one?

BEN: Eating. Or in the bathroom. Or taking an urgent call from his family.

TINA: So, contrary to science and common sense, cops actually eat, pee, have sex and make families. I can't understand.

BEN: So that's it? Fine. End of discussion. Let 'em fuck you. When they ask, I'll say the cops did all they could to keep them from attacking you, but not even you cared.

TINA: You see why I don't want you talking to reporters or digging around in blogs?

BEN: Why?

TINA: The drama, darling.

BEN: So these people who want to kill you they can't come a couple of days before and study the cops' routines and, right when this one's eating and that one's fucking the neighbor, and the other one's talking to his family, the professional terrorists pull up with their Kalashnikovs and: bang bang bang! And it's lights out for star editor of The Viral Vampire and heroine of the civilized world. Tina "Teeny Tiny" Galloway!

TINA: Stop calling me that, pet names are insulting. And they won't say Tina Galloway. They'll say formerly Galloway. Ex Galloway, they'll say. You think you can do something to get them to change my name?

BEN: Once you're dead, no chance.

TINA: Getting killed this way in a terrorist attack condemned by the civilized world and getting stuck with the name Tina, should be off limits even for the truly depraved.

BEN: Don't worry, sweetheart. Seeing as you're so ex, maybe you'll end up an ex-Tina, someone who no longer exists.

TINA: Yes. An ex. Ex-Tina. Ex-Galloway. Ex-fucking victim.

BEN: Of an ex-Kalashnikov in an ex-attack and now extremely ex-dead.

TINA: Quit being so jumpy. My death hasn't been planned out in that much detail.

BEN: That's not what they're saying online, chéri.

TINA: Remember, bad guys are idiots.

BEN: Yes, but, who are the bad guys?

TINA: Them, the idiots.

BEN: I'm not saying they're anything to brag about but with the police protection you've got, it won't take a genius to come and…

TINA: Pump me full of lead.

BEN: Pump you full of lead.

TINA: You like picturing it, don't you?

BEN: No, I don't like picturing it, stupid.

TINA: I didn't realize you cared so much, ex-husband.

BEN: I don't, ex-wife. It's just when they come to do it, I might get caught in the crossfire and a fine, upstanding Christian will end up paying for a godless sinner like you.

TINA: Don't worry. I made a deal with my killers. They'll make sure you're not around when they come to carry out their contract. They promised to kill me all by my lonesome. They'll rape me first, of course, and then the Kalashnikovs. You know they adore me.

BEN: How thoughtful. I feel so much better.

TINA: Besides, the terrorists know perfectly well you won't defend me.

BEN: *(Suddenly serious)* Of course I'd defend you, Tina. You're you: my wife, mother of my child. I'd defend you, you idiotic idiot. Of course I would. With my life.

TINA: Don't go all Hallmark on me, darling. Admit it: if the big bad criminals come and ask, you'll tell them where I am, what I'm doing, the location of my secret hiding places, the best time for me to die and where I'd like the Kalashnikov's bullet holes. At least one in the forehead, you'll recommend.

BEN: Fine. It's true. I won't defend you. But I won't do their work for them either. I'll run screaming like a madman: "they're killing her," "they're gunning her down" and then I'll give a statement to the press. You have no idea how badly I want to play the famous widower, basking in society's pity for the man who gave his all for the victim. That'll wipe out my online history. I'll leave the scandal completely behind. From that day search engines will remember me as the widower who saw how they mowed down his wife, who tried his best to save her but couldn't, and afterward got everything. A black widower, they'll say. At your funeral, I'll quote that bit about how you had your whole life ahead of you and how your terrifying killers and their bullets won't stop your work, the weekly Viral Vampire. How that loathsome Vampire will go on protecting freedom of speech, as the most searched for entertainment site on the web with all the sex, blood, stupidity, racism, fundamentalism and hate anyone could hope for.

TINA: No, you won't say that.

BEN: I will. And since I'll be left in charge of your blog, I'll shut down that sleazy Vampire the next month.

TINA: Why? It's a great business!

BEN: So great you need three cops to protect you?

TINA: Because I don't plan to die of neglect. Can you hand me my pills?

(Ben picks up the pills, but hangs on to them, studying the label carefully)

BEN: Are these new?

TINA: They're the same.

BEN: It says 500 mg.

TINA: Can I have them please?

BEN: You used to take 250 mg.

TINA: And I used to take two.

BEN: Now it's two at 500.

TINA: It's the same.

BEN: It is?

TINA: Math is impenetrable, darling. …

(She takes the bottle, opens it and takes two pills)

BEN: And you swallow two of them?

TINA: They upped my dose, Ben. What's with you? Since when do you care about my meds? You planning to poison me? Because I won't let you. It's the Kalashnikovs for me, noise, commotion. Poisoned like a holdover from the 20th century? No sir. Dead, but contemporary.

BEN: I never did know what's hurting you, exactly.

TINA: You don't need to.

BEN: I just wanted an idea.

TINA: Honestly… You care?

BEN: Of course I care, I'm not an animal!

TINA: Of course you're an animal.

BEN: Where'd you get that idea?

TINA: From last week's op-ed in The Post, which states, unequivocally, that anyone who wants to hurt me is an animal. They're not just against me, a human being, by the way. They're against the country, our freedoms, the whole Western tradition even.

BEN: I disagree. A desire to hurt you doesn't automatically make someone an animal. In my case, it's more of an intellectual reaction. After weighing facts and memories and considering the good of the whole versus the individual, while taking into account the circumstances and your face, I quite logically reached a rational conclusion that could be considered scientific. Namely: someone needs to hurt you.

TINA: Kill me.

BEN: No, of course not.

TINA: Then what?

BEN: Hurt you, that's all.

TINA: And that's it.

BEN: The necessary amount. But no more.

TINA: Are you sure you're not the one writing the speeches for those animals?

BEN: Darling, it's my understanding, as well as public knowledge, that you do that yourself.

TINA: You're absurd.

(Ben takes the pills from Tina.)

BEN: Absurd is popping pills like Tic Tacs.

TINA: I've been at this new dose for a month, Ben.

BEN: A month? I didn't know.

TINA: You didn't know? Well, what do you know?

BEN: Nothing, I know nothing.

(Ben moves away carefully, like someone crossing quicksand.)

TINA: Oh! I get it! You think they upped my dosage because it was when we made our decision. Is that it?

BEN: It crossed my mind.

TINA: It's not that I've gotten eleven death threats. No. That couldn't be important. The main thing is that a month ago we decided to get divorced and that's why the pain got worse. That's me: I need you so so much.

BEN: Of course you don't need me, Tina.

TINA: You thought it! I saw it in your face when you took the pills. You gave yourself away, Ben.

BEN: How'd I give myself away?

TINA: Your eyes. They get all squinty.

BEN: My eyes don't get squinty…!

TINA: Of course they do. When you feel guilty, it's not just your eyes that shrink up. It's your legs, your shoulders, your back hunches. Guilt takes at least two inches off you. We've been married twenty years, darling. Remember, you're the main character in my life. Not me. In my life I'm just the sidekick. In this show, you're the big shot.

BEN: Maybe you shouldn't mention shots, the cops aren't protecting us.

TINA: They're not protecting me!

(Tina primps at the mirror.)

BEN: Tina, I didn't say our divorce was causing your pain. Pain is pain. It's not necessarily from that. If they doubled your dose, it must be because you need it. That's all. I'm not nosing into your business and it's abundantly clear that in your movie the leading lady is you. In fact, your life's not a movie, it's a viral video.

TINA: Now that's a compliment.

BEN: A video monologue, more like.

TINA: How sweet.

BEN: Like they ones Nicole used to do.

(Pause. Nicole's name affects Tina.)

TINA: What do you think she's doing now?

BEN: Having coffee with one of her friends.

TINA: She's not all that crazy about coffee. She's probably watching TV, killing time before getting ready for a party.

BEN: On a Monday?

TINA: Monday parties. It's probably what kids are into these days.

BEN: Ok. But she doesn't watch TV. She listens to music.

TINA: Right. Music.

BEN: And she blurts out the lyrics before the singer.

TINA: She'll drive you crazy, that girl.

BEN: Remember how she used to change the words to get our attention?

TINA: To make us correct her! But she always knew them.

BEN: She knew them all by heart.

TINA: How'd she do that?

BEN: Repetition. At her age, they listen over and over. Period.

TINA: Maybe today she's going to the mall with her best friends.

BEN: And they'll talk the day away.

TINA: Make fun of the people going by.

BEN: Horse around…

TINA: Laughing and shushing each other, all of them at once.

(About to laugh)

BEN: And taking ridiculous selfies.

TINA: Stupid pictures.

BEN: It's just…

TINA: Her and her sarcasm…

BEN: That irony…

TINA: And her laugh…

BEN: Oh my god, that laugh!

TINA: Scanning a dozen store windows a second. There's no way she can see all that. But she does!

BEN: Impossible.

TINA: An impossible girl.

BEN: Not a girl. She's twenty. She's a young woman now.

TINA: You think she still smokes?

BEN: Still? She smoked before?

TINA: She was already buying cigarettes at fifteen.

BEN: Really?

TINA: That's why she didn't want a ride to school.

BEN: Because she smoked!

TINA: From the time she hit fifteen she was really rebellious, you know that.

BEN: She smoked alone?

TINA: With her best friend, that weird girlfriend of hers.

BEN: She wasn't weird...

TINA: Of course she was weird.

BEN: So just cigarettes or other stuff?

TINA: She might've tried soft drugs. I don't know... pot maybe.

BEN: You think that's why she...?

TINA: If that's why?

BEN: Yeah, that.

TINA: If she ran away because of drugs and all that?

BEN: It could be. Right?

TINA: No, no way. Nicole's always been very independent. Remember when she was five how she packed a bag, opened the door and off she went, just like that?

BEN: (*Laughing*) I had to go chasing after her!

TINA: We put special locks on the door!

BEN: All kids do that. Run off. Explore. It's natural.

TINA: But when she was ten Nicole used to talk about taking off and living her life without us. Then, when she was twelve she got the big idea to run off to L.A. Remember? "To try her luck" she said. The dream,

Hollywood, stardom. She was twelve! *(Imitating her)* "I'll go to auditions, get an agent. I'll give it three years. If I don't make it, I'll go somewhere else, the beach, work in a bar or a surf shop." She even wanted to change her name!

BEN: Whose name?

TINA: The dog's, stupid. Her last name.

BEN: My name? Galloway?

TINA: It was any last name, whether you gave it to her or I did… It's symbolic, what the last name stands for. And she didn't just want to change her last name, she wanted to change her first name too. *(Mimicking her)* "Don't call me Nicole. It sounds like a Disney princess. I want a name with personality."

BEN: You're going a bit overboard with her tone.

TINA: That's how she talked! Exactly like that.

BEN: With that retarded little voice?

TINA: It was our fault. We didn't make her watch enough classic movies.

BEN: Because they were all about warrior princesses and you thought it would make her gay.

TINA: Well I was right in the end. Wasn't I?

BEN: The end?

TINA: I mean she ran off with her girlfriend.

BEN: Yes, but that doesn't mean "the end."

TINA: Well, I would've liked some grandchildren, like any mother.

BEN: And gay women can't have kids?

TINA: The point is we women need more positive messages.

BEN: What would Nicole say about all this?

TINA: All what?

BEN: What would she say about our separation?

TINA: It's not a separation, it's a divorce.

BEN: A big one.

TINA: The only one you'll remember in your life, Ben.

(Tina goes back to her iPad. Ben looks at himself in the mirror. He touches some wrinkles near his eyes. He dabs on moisturizer.)

BEN: So that's it. Today I find out my daughter always wanted to run off, she smoked when she was a kid, she didn't want my last name, and Disney movies make little girls gay. And you decide to tell me all this after we've been married for twenty years, sweetheart?

TINA: *(Puts on her reading glasses and picks up the folder)* Since we're dividing up our assets I figured we should do the same with the secrets we've been keeping. That way there's nothing left and later there's no arguing over who gets what: bank accounts, cars, house, secrets. Divvy it all up.

BEN: Memories.

TINA: Same thing, darling: secrets, memories, garbage.

BEN: Are you saying you have more secrets? Or did you just concoct a couple to try and convince me I don't know you from the tip of your big toe to the last curl on your head?

TINA: Of course I do.

BEN: Like what?

TINA: Like, about Nicole.

BEN: More secrets about Nicole!

TINA: She's the center of everything, isn't she?

BEN: I thought you were the center of everything.

TINA: I'm above the center. Let's just say I'm the one who divvies up the centers.

BEN: Just like you're divvying up our separation. All right, what other secrets do you have on your list of marital assets?

TINA: *(Ben, waiting)* You remember I said I didn't see her that morning?

BEN: That morning?

TINA: The morning of that animal.

BEN: That was five years ago, sweetheart.

TINA: Five whole years! Incredible.

BEN: The secret?

TINA: I always said that you and I were here in the bathroom at 11 a.m. and that I never saw her leave.

BEN: Leave us.

TINA: Just like that.

BEN: It's true. And for the record, you always say it in that soap opera voice.

TINA: Well…

BEN: That's not how it was?

TINA: Technically, no.

BEN: Technically?

TINA: I left out a few details.

BEN: What happened?

(Ben begins shaving, automatically.)

TINA: At one point, when I was alone, I heard a noise outside and I saw her from the window here.

BEN: You saw her? Outside?

TINA: Leaving. Ditching us.

BEN: What did you see?

TINA: She had her backpack and she was wearing her yellow dress. She ran out to a car and there was that girl, waiting for her.

BEN: What girl?

TINA: Her girlfriend. Andrea? Adriana? That bitch. She was wearing a Yankees cap. Who does that? You could see them plain as day from the bathroom window.

BEN: What kind of car? A new one?

TINA: A Corolla. Old. Red. And that…woman took her away.

BEN: We already knew that, Tiny.

TINA: Yeah, it's just that…the secret is I saw her out the window and I always swore I hadn't.

BEN: Tina, whether you saw her or not isn't relevant.

TINA: She ran off with that idiot.

BEN: You're making chicken salad out of feathers.

TINA: I'm making chicken soup?

BEN: Your story's got no meat, sweetheart. *(Ben stops shaving)* Mine's better. *(Like he's about to say something amazing)* I ran into the Fuentes yesterday.

TINA: That little slut's parents? Those pigs next door? What did that trash say to you?

BEN: Five years later and we just chatted like nothing had happened. After a while I had to bring it up: what do you know about the girls? Like they were a couple of neighborhood kids. Her mom said someone had seen them at the beach, in Florida, apparently. In a snorkel shop. They were doing fine, she said.

TINA: Of course they're fine! When you don't love anyone, you're always fine.

BEN: Her dad said he'd seen a TV show about runaways. Said lots of times it's got nothing to do with the parents. It's their environment. Maybe they hate the city, or their school, and then one talks the other into it and…

TINA: Is that what that son of a bitch said to you?

BEN: He insinuated that Nicole had talked his daughter into it.

TINA: Right, the bad influence of a fifteen-year-old girl on an eighteen-year-old bitch who should be in jail for seducing a minor. Did you mention that to him?

BEN: He also said the clues to a runaway are in what they said and did the day before.

TINA: Sounds simple.

BEN: You know what they're like and where they're from.

TINA: What did she say and do the day before? Nothing. Nicole didn't do anything special the day before. She went to school, listened to music. Fought with me. Smoked whatever. Online all day talking to her trashy girlfriend and up till three in the morning. The usual, completely normal. And the next day: backpack, blue dress, and a red Corolla.

BEN: That's what I figured. But now I'm wondering: why didn't you tell me you saw her leave? *(She doesn't answer)* Tina, tell me: are you stupid?

TINA: I'm not stupid.

BEN: So? Why aren't you answering me?

TINA: Was that an actual question or just rhetorical?

BEN: What possible importance can it have, Tina?

TINA: Forget it.

BEN: Tell me.

TINA: What?

BEN: Why'd you lie about something so stupid?

TINA: Huh?

BEN: *(Serious)* Why hide something so trivial? Tell me!

TINA: Because she didn't look back!

BEN: Who?

TINA: *(Suddenly, angry)* She didn't even look back! She tossed her bag in the back of the Corolla, got in, kissed that little slut and not once did she look back at her house, to say goodbye to the walls, to the doors or at least to me, watching her from the window. I told myself: if she turns to look for me she'll come back. I told myself that: if she looks back, it'll be like a goodbye and it will make it all meaningful. But that's not how it went. She didn't even glance at her home! She left for good, or at least for five years, and she couldn't even lift a finger to say: *(Imitating Nicole)* "I should leave my parents a note so they won't worry about me!" *(Ben disapproves of her imitation)* That's why I never mentioned I saw her leave. Because it felt too harsh, too humiliating. Better to leave the mystery, right? She left and we don't know where she is!

(Ben moves away from her, stands in front of the Hopper.)

BEN: Do you mind if I take this poster?

TINA: What do you want that for?

BEN: You want me to leave it for you?

TINA: I can't even remember when we hung it there.

BEN: I got it years ago on my trip to Osaka. We hung it in a few other spots then banished it here.

TINA: What do you like about it anyway? A woman looking out the window?

BEN: The art of looking. Pondering the idea of leaning in. Seeing the other.

TINA: What's it called?

BEN: Eleven a.m. It's what Hopper does. He calls it The August Feeling. Feeling excited about change, about the idea that your life has meaning in relation to others.

TINA: That all seems kind of abstract to me.

BEN: That's Hopper: reality as abstraction.

TINA: Ben, I've always thought that painting was ugly. If you want to take it, go ahead.

BEN: What else do we need to divvy up, sweetheart, so we can get this Kalashnikov divorce over with?

TINA: You need to sign Nicole's trust fund.

BEN: You left it on the iPad?

TINA: No, it's over here… (Takes a folder from the counter and hands it to him) I already signed.

BEN: You think it's enough?

TINA: It's a decent amount. Nicole will see it as an advance on her inheritance. At her age she'll be able to do whatever she wants.

BEN: But we didn't give her the option of the house.

TINA: That was your idea.

BEN: Yours. Your idea.

TINA: It just makes sense. The house has built-in security, planned escape routes, everything all ready and rehearsed for the day of the attacks that will finish me off. So, I'm keeping the house. Nicole gets money and that's it.

BEN: Tell me the truth: why do you want to stay here?

TINA: The truth? Fine. (Pauses, like someone about to reveal an important truth) Because it would really piss off the guys who are gonna kill me. If they came looking for me and found out I don't live here anymore. My killers would hate me.

BEN: We could leave them a little note with instructions: "Dear Terrorists, dearest friends, your victim has moved. Please, forward your plan to kill her in the night to such and such address."

TINA: Or maybe we can ask the cops to escort them. We wouldn't want the poor terrorists to get lost. These suburban streets can be very dangerous.

BEN: *(Gesturing around him, serious)* I'm really going to miss it.

TINA: Forget about the house, Ben. In any case, if I die, which could happen any second if these killers weren't so lame, you won't get the house. In my will, I left it to Nicole and her LG-BLT descendants, if she has any.

BEN: Sweetheart: they're never going to kill you. I never did and look at all the chances I've had.

TINA: Don't overestimate yourself. You're useless and you know it.

BEN: I'm serious.

TINA: I'm serious! We're talking about death, aren't we?! What's more serious than that? Or at least about killing, which in my case is the same thing.

BEN: Let's agree on one thing—you're not going to die of natural causes any time soon. By the time you start to go, poor Nicole will be watching our grandkids graduate from college! She won't need the house then.

TINA: A house always make a difference, chéri.

(She starts to dress. He does too.)

BEN: And Vampire's yours.

TINA: What about it?

BEN: Just that it's yours.

TINA: Isn't it mine?

BEN: In the beginning it belonged to both of us…

TINA: Ben, Vampire is mine. I thought that was clear. Because I don't see your name on any death threats. There's no Kalashnikov with your face etched in its steel grip.

(Ben goes to her, serious. He strokes her arm.)

BEN: Tina, I want to know…

TINA: A Kalashnikov question?

BEN: Yes, a Kalashnikov question.

TINA: Do you have to touch me to ask it?

BEN: No, but I like touching you.

TINA: *(Removing his hand)* Just ask.

BEN: You know the strange thing about clocks?

TINA: What, they run slow on purpose?

BEN: Pendulum clocks. If you set two of them with their pendulums swinging in opposite directions, after a while they'll synchronize, without anyone touching them.

TINA: I don't understand.

BEN: The phenomenon happens with all oscillators. Even in nature: between fireflies, heart cells…

TINA: *(Fed up)* So? What's your point?

BEN: And most likely between us.

TINA: What, we'll end up synchronized? Is that it?

BEN: It happens with clocks.

TINA: But, darling, your timing's always been lousy.

(We hear noises in the distance. A siren approaching. Police radios. Tina and Ben grow nervous. She goes to leave, but he pulls her back protectively and shuts the door.)

BEN: What?! What is that?

TINA: The killers?

BEN: Are they here?

TINA: Oh my god! What? What's going on?

BEN: Someone's moving around out there! *(He leans toward the window)* Two more cop cars just pulled up! And an ambulance!

TINA: Oh god! An ambulance! Are you sure? God, god, god!

(Tina takes the Superman t-shirt and hugs it to her chest protectively.)

BEN: What are you doing?

TINA: If they're going to kill me, I want them to find me with it!

BEN: They're not going to kill you today!

TINA: How do you know?

BEN: Because it's the cops!

TINA: The cops don't make me feel any better, Ben! They're all for sale! They hate the Vampire!

BEN: Don't be stupid!

TINA: I'm not stupid!

BEN: Then what?

TINA: I'm terrified, they're different things!

BEN: Calm down, nothing's going to happen to you!

TINA: Oh god, Ben! Oh god!

(Tina's cell phone rings and immediately after, Ben's. Then the landline in the bathroom rings. Both go to it.)

BEN: Who could it be?

TINA: Make sure the recorder and tracing system are on!

BEN: They are!

TINA: Then, pick up!

BEN: Me?

TINA: Yes, you.

BEN: Why?

TINA: Because maybe they're waiting for me to answer and then they'll shoot me through the window.

BEN: What if they shoot me?

TINA: No one wants to kill you!

BEN: It doesn't feel that way to me! *(Ben answers)* Hello? Detective Pineda? *(Listens)* We're both in the bathroom. When we heard the sirens we shut the security door and moved away from the window. *(Listens)* There's one in the bathroom, but it's off.

TINA: *(Nervous)* What is? What's off?

BEN: *(To Tina)* The TV. Pineda says not to turn it on. Don't do anything. He's on his way here... *(To the phone)* Yes? I promise we won't watch the TV before you get here...But tell me: what's going on? *(Tina goes and turns on the TV)* He said not to do that!

TINA: No one tells me what to do!

(Ben fights with her over the remote, but Tina wins. When Ben is about to turn the TV off manually, we hear the news.)

TV: According to a police source, the lifeless bodies of Nicole Galloway and Adriana Fuentes, missing for five years, were found in the backyard of Tina Galloway's own home. The journalist and blogger, editor of controversial online magazine The Viral Vampire, has received as many as eleven death threats from different domestic and international organizations...

(The chorus of Elton John's "Tiny Dancer" plays. Black out.)

2 /

(In video, we see Detective Pineda speaking into a microphone or recorder. Above him, a digital clock with large numbers displays the time as 1:45 p.m. *Instead of a video, this effect can also be done with voices offstage.)

PINEDA: *(Off/video)* Detective Jacinto Pineda, Homicide. Statement on the double murder case of Nicole Galloway and Adriana Fuentes. Interview with Benjamin Galloway, father of Nicole Galloway, in the presence of his lawyer... *(Motions for the lawyer to state his name.)*

LAWYER: *(Off/video)* Alex Rodgers...

PINEDA: *(Off/video)* Let's begin...

(When the lights come up onstage, we see Ben, alone. Beside him, a microphone or recorder with a red light on. In the distance, we see Tina dimly, getting ready in the bathroom. The digital clock now shows the time as 3:07 p.m.)

BEN: The last time I saw her was that morning, five years ago. She was walking from her room to the kitchen. I warned her not to go outside because of what was going on. She said she'd stay in her room until everything was safe. That's the last thing I heard her say and, as you know, I never saw her again.
(Short pause as he listens then answers.)
She was with her friend, Adriana. They'd had a sleepover, they did that a lot. They'd stay up talking and then she'd sleep over at the house. At first, it seemed normal. We were neighbors, you know? But then we

realized, just by watching because they never told us, that the relationship between the two of them was, let's just say, more than friendly. *(Listens)* Yes, they were lovers. *(Listens)* Uh...Well, we didn't exactly jump for joy at the news, but we saw it as a thing kids do.
(Short pause as he listens then answers)
My computer? I heard you took it from the house. *(Listens)* Porn? I guess I've watched porn now and then, yeah. *(Listens)* No, porn doesn't have anything to do with our divorce. We've been married twenty years and... *(Listens)* Yeah, sure, the magazine's caused problems, safety issues let's say. We have to live with three cops 24 hours a day! But that hasn't affected our home life. *(Listens)* Another woman? *(Listens)* The Japanese letters. You saw those? Well, that was a long time ago, detective.
(Short pause. Ben steels himself.)
It happened in Osaka, at a video game conference. We got seated next to each other. We talked, but we didn't understand each other. We said things anyway and acted like we understood and laughed a lot. We looked at each other a lot too, like trying to say things. We went out every night, we slept together for a whole week and I nearly stayed in Japan for her. And still, I never learned her name. Ociko, Nariko, Dorito, what do I know?! In the end, all she got was my email address, that's it. She still writes me those long letters you saw on the computer. I don't answer, because for one thing, I can't write in Japanese and I don't understand what she writes either. I know they're from her, but honestly they could be from anyone. Maybe it's spam. My lovesick spam. Of course, you can't really consider that an affair, strictly speaking. Though when I'm sitting by my wife, without her realizing or me looking at her, I pretend I'm with my Japanese woman and I picture scenes from my happy life, or complicated life, but a life with the stranger whose name I never even knew, or what she said to me, or what she was like, or what she believed. And in the end, she had no idea who I was either. Maybe that's

happiness. When they don't know you, they don't understand you, but they stay with you anyway.
(Ben looks around for Tina. He's interrupted by Pineda. He listens and answers.)
Back then I was composing video game soundtracks. Yeah, you could say I was well-known. You could also say I had my enemies. You know, if people like to throw around insults online, I won't even get into how nasty the fans of sim games can get! That's why we say getting offended and being innocent at the same time is our culture's worst vice.
(Listens) The games simulate family life, work, friends, city, hobbies, talents, hook-ups, cheating, things to do, all of it. The player picks a personality and a body, though it's almost always the other way around: first the body, then the personality. We've done studies and apparently it's an instinct.
(Listens) No, I never received any death threats over the scandal I was mixed up in. Though…um…how should I put this?
(Rapid-fire, professional) Look, in this business, we celebrate narcissism. If we killed God in the 20th century, in the 21st we killed the Other, other people. People are anxious to be known, to leverage their successes, to keep up appearances. We can't breathe if we're irrelevant.
So, that narcissistic drive gives birth to a kind of visceral rage, without intellectual processing. An emotional outrage that takes any little thing and turns it into conflict.
(Listens) Yes, of course it's occurred to me. That someone who hated me for the scandal with the video game soundtrack could've killed my daughter and the other girl that morning. For narcisso-emotional revenge, let's say.
(Suddenly one of Pineda's questions riles him.)
What? *(Listens)* The anonymous tip?
(Listens) No, I don't know who told you where to find the bodies of my daughter and her friend.

135

(Listens) Really? You think I know something? *(Listens)* You think it was me? *(Stands, angry)* That I called to tell you where my daughter's body was? And why would I do a thing like that? *(Listens)* Secrets? Have you lost your mind?

(Music. Five years ago. Master bathroom in the Galloway house. 11 a.m. Tina runs in holding binoculars. She's more attractive and fresher than in the previous scene. She's wearing the Superman t-shirt. She goes to the window.)

TINA: You have to come see this! Hurry Ben! He could be gone before we get a picture! *(Looking through the binoculars)* Unbelievable. Unbelievable. This town is unbelievable!

(Enter Ben with bigger binoculars. He's dressed for work.)

BEN: You'll see it better with these.

TINA: But, is it or isn't it?

BEN: Sure looks like it.

TINA: Jesus Christ! But… What's it doing? *(Looks through the binoculars again)* Wait, I think it's moving!

BEN: It's not moving…It's not doing anything, Tina.

TINA: But… Who? Who would dump that here?

BEN: *(Looking through the window again)* Now it is moving!

TINA: Let me see! *(Takes the binoculars)* Oh my god, what if it gets inside?

BEN: It's not getting inside. The house is closed up.

TINA: But, what if it does?

BEN: I already called the police, Tina. You need to calm down.

TINA: Nicole?

BEN: In her room. She won't go out till everything's safe. Remember she's rebellious, but she's chicken too.

TINA: But, do you know what kind it is?

BEN: I think it's some kind of lizard.

TINA: Are you sure? A lizard? Not a crocodile? Or maybe an enormous snake? Anaconda? An anaconda! I saw the movie. Those things eat everything!

BEN: It doesn't look like a snake, sweetheart.

TINA: Even people. In the movie it ate a whole bunch of them and kept them all alive until it tore them apart by slithering around. Yeah, maybe it's a boa constrictor.

BEN: Look at the size of her, Tina. She's too fat to be a reptile.

TINA: She? It's female?

BEN: I just called it that.

TINA: The he-croc is a she-croc or the he-constrictor is a she-constrictor?

BEN: Whatever it is, it's too fat to be a snake.

TINA: Maybe it ate someone and that's why it's so big.

BEN: I'm telling you, it's a lizard.

TINA: Then explain this to me: where did a crocodile that size come from and how did it get outside my front door?!

BEN: Lizards and crocodiles aren't the same thing, Tina.

TINA: To me they're all the same monster!

BEN: I agree with you there. But it doesn't look dangerous. It looks like it's resting.

TINA: Maybe it's never seen humans?

BEN: Or at least not you.

TINA: Very funny.

BEN: I meant you're easy pickings.

TINA: I'm not easy pickings. That's what I wanted you to think. Which just goes to show I'm not easy at all. Are you sure it's not some other kind of snake?

BEN: *(Both look through the binoculars)* Take a good look at the palm tree. See it? Ok, now look at the lizard. Proportionally, you see the size?

TINA: It's huge

BEN: Right. Maybe it escaped from the zoo.

TINA: You think it's trained?

BEN: As far as I know you can't train a lizard.

TINA: But maybe you can train a crocodile.

BEN: No way! And it's not a lizard! I mean, it's not a crocodile!

TINA: Are you saying all we can do is feed the thing?

BEN: They have their schedules. If it already ate, it won't bother us.

TINA: Already ate where?

BEN: It has to be from the zoo.

TINA: So it escaped?

BEN: It's happened. Lizards who've lived their whole lives in the zoo and suddenly they escape.

TINA: So you're saying they're not wild animals.

BEN: All they do is sleep all day.

TINA: Why don't you go check and see if it's sleeping or if it's hungry? I'll watch over you from here.

BEN: No, thanks, I prefer not to disturb other people when they're sleeping.

TINA: People? Try monster! A monster that's hunting us I'd say.

BEN: We're safe here.

TINA: You're not going to the office?

BEN: I think today I have a very good excuse for being late.

TINA: This, Ben, is a prime excuse.

BEN: And verifiable. I bet it'll be on the news.

TINA: (*Excited, looking out the window*) Have you seen reporters?

BEN: No, but they'll come.

TINA: To confirm your alibi!

BEN: It's the truth!

TINA: Exactly. A perfect excuse. If you'd told me last week that you couldn't make it home because you were trapped in the office by a reptile, or a tiger, or poisonous bees, now that would've been a serious excuse. Imaginary, but excellent. Instead, the excuse you made, darling: no press, no lizard, no nothing.

BEN: I couldn't make it home because Marketing found a glitch in the video game soundtrack. I had to fix it for the TV spot. That's why I stayed. I told you, you know it and it's true.

TINA: Marketing and music aren't the same as a crocodile lizard anaconda parked outside your office door.

BEN: It's pretty much the same. It's an obstacle.

TINA: Shut in all night, cornered by a cholesterol crocodile blocking the only exit, like a sniper, only not with bullets, with teeth, so you have to spend the night with your Japanese assistant. What's her name, Burrito?

BEN: My assistant?

TINA: I'm talking about the anaconda.

BEN: My assistant isn't Japanese, Tina.

TINA: Chinese? Filipina?

BEN: You're mixing her up.

TINA: I'm not mixing her up. Remember I found her love letter on your iPad! *(Tina goes to his iPad and searches.)*

BEN: You didn't find any letter.

TINA: *(She finds it)* Here it is! In Japanese!

BEN: It's not a love letter.

TINA: Maybe it is. Anyway, I don't read Japanese and the online dictionary chops it all up and I can't understand crap.

BEN: My assistant is Nari Ok and she's from Korea.

TINA: Right. With Narico, Bimbico, Burrito, and the anaconda with an alibi.

BEN: There's no alibi! There's no anaconda! There's no Burrito! Bimbico! Nari Ok! My assistant works on the soundtracks with me, that's it. Our work is public. You checked that day online and saw it was true: press preview of the trailer for the new sim game. "Ben Galloway's soundtrack was glitchy," just like I said.

TINA: Glitchy? They said glitchy?

BEN: That it needed fixing.

TINA: *(Tina goes back to the iPad)* Let's check again.

BEN: Seriously, Tina?

TINA: You're the famous one. It's your name on the internet. You're the one they hate.

BEN: They don't hate me.

TINA: Ben, I search your name on Google every day.

BEN: You shouldn't...

TINA: They detest you.

BEN: Don't be silly...

TINA: You're more famous than the black and gold dress. Or keyboard cat. Some memes even stick your head on the cat's body!

BEN: God that's humiliating. Please, don't remind me.

TINA: Darling, you're the must-see trend for all that venom.

BEN: Don't exaggerate. It's over.

TINA: Over? Not even close!

BEN: It was a blip. (*Gets an idea*) You think maybe, because of all those complaints about me, someone dumped a lizard on our doorstep?

TINA: Could be. When the cops confiscated your computer it made you look really bad...

BEN: I had my whole life on that PC!

TINA: You had porn!

BEN: Everyone has porn!

TINA: I don't!

BEN: Well I do!

TINA: And you looked guilty.

BEN: Where? Where'd I look guilty?

TINA: Online. (*Tina looking at her iPad*) Look, here's a tweet.

BEN: What?

TINA: One of your haters. And the search brought him up fast: 0.041 seconds.

BEN: It's trolls, they fuck with you over anything. And being offensive gets likes so their posts go viral faster and they look like a lot of people. But they're not. They're not real.

TINA: 0.041 seconds of hate looks real to me.

BEN: *(Checks his own iPad)* Where's it say?

TINA: For example, @mcmann, in Miami, despises you. Reeeaally. He calls you A soulless Bozo. Bozo was a popular clown back in…

BEN: You don't have to treat me like an idiot, Tina.

TINA: Another one tells you to go to hell, but in 0.045 seconds, some @frankpollard, in Australia…

BEN: They have no reason to hate me…

TINA: In 0.051 seconds @musicpolice, in New York uses the hashtag #BenGallowayplagiarist. Wow, kid's blunt. Says your video soundtrack is copied from Tchaikovsky, Bach and ten others. Plagiarism times ten, Ben?

BEN: Give me a fucking break. They're classics.

TINA: And you take credit for them. Don't you think it's kind of arrogant to take credit like you're a classic?

BEN: I don't copy. I reread.

(Ben checks what Tina is pointing to. They face each other, in the same position, holding their respective iPads.)

TINA: You reread so much you end up copying. I have an open letter from Mozarteum calling for someone, anyone to slit your throat in the town square. There's even a link on Wikipedia. The Beethoven Foundation is calling for your head. And the Wagnerians, you know what Nazis they are, they want the gas chamber. No imagination, honestly.

BEN: Who me? I have no imagination?

TINA: They posted a picture of you with a Hitler mustache. And the two of you as cats playing an eight-pawed duet on the piano.

BEN: No matter what you do you end up with mortal enemies online.

TINA: The Stravinsky non-profit, which I understand is extremely dangerous, has asked for you to be drawn and quartered for plagiarism. Why do they use plagiarism and kidnapping like they're interchangeable?

BEN: I didn't kidnap anyone.

TINA: *(Reads on the iPad)* Wow your fans are really reblogging the kidnapping hashtag. You're trending. #BenGallowayplagiarist is popping up even in China and Japan. That's where they despise you the most, it looks like. You think it could be one of Burrito's boyfriends behind all this?

BEN: Leave Taquito alone! Nari Ok!

TINA: *(Reads)* "Ben Galloway's soundtracks are crap." This is a whole blog dedicated to you.

BEN: A blog? Son of a bitch. Where?

TINA: *(Reads)* #BenGallowayplagiarist: Debussy copies.

BEN: They're not copies!

TINA: #BenGallowayplagiarist: Refried Schubert.

BEN: It says refried... son of a bitch...

TINA: #BenGallowayplagiarist: Chopin too.

BEN: He's Romantic, it's confusing.

TINA: Like love songs?

BEN: Sort of, but they're not...

TINA: So slow dancing and making out is what this Chopin guy is good for.

BEN: They're dreams, recollections, inspirations, versions, adaptations, nods, hints, tributes.

TINA: But tell me, is it true? Do you copy?

BEN: Huh?

TINA: Tell me right now, do you plagiarize? Kidnap?

BEN: Of course not, stupid!

TINA: So you hint. Meaning, they're similar.

BEN: Who?

TINA: Your music and theirs.

BEN: They're all similar.

TINA: Similar as in imitation.

BEN: Nothing's original.

TINA: You know what I mean.

BEN: It's my job.

TINA: And the copy's worth money.

BEN: Inspiration.

TINA: Traced, duplicated...

BEN: A nod to...

TINA: Transcribed, plagiarized.

BEN: A version of...

TINA: And are they like the good ones or are they...?

BEN: An approximation...

TINA: Shit.

BEN: What?

TINA: I asked are they shit.

BEN: Of course they're not shit! They're good!

TINA: How do you know?

BEN: Because I make money off them!

TINA: But that's not what these sites say. For example: (*Looks on her iPad*) 1.12 seconds. "What's more predictable: the game or the music?"

BEN: It's not...

TINA: (*Reads*) Ben Galloway composes like he's cranking the handle on a player piano churning out tinny, predictable notes almost good enough to play in a whorehouse waiting room." Hah?

BEN: They don't know what they're talking about...

TINA: "Airport and elevator muzak sounds like jazz or the Beatles after listening to Ben Galloway's bland and pompous copies..."

BEN: An unfounded opinion...

TINA: They call you pompous...

BEN: Another word for complex. I'm sure it's just one person saying that...

TINA: @missvero in Ecuador, @tatianapeters, in Virginia, @lucilleasp in L.A. And they're all very happy to share the hashtag #BenGallowayplagiarist.

BEN: You're making that up.

TINA: I'm not. The thing is I didn't know, Ben.

BEN: What? Didn't know what?

TINA: I didn't know you're shit.

BEN: I am not shit!

(Tina sets her iPad down and singsongs.)

TINA: #BenGallowayplagiarist.

(Ben goes to the mirror again, clearly thinking he's about to win the argument.)

BEN: Ask Nicole.

TINA: Nicole?

BEN: She loves our sim. *(Now definitely more assured of his victory)* She's really proud of me. She brags to her friends. I've signed games for several of them, including her girlfriend.

TINA: Even though they hate you all over the web for being a kidnapping, talentless, plagiarizing shit?

BEN: They admire me for it. They call me "badass."

TINA: What's that supposed to mean…?

BEN: I'm shameless.

TINA: That's it: integrity is dead.

BEN: Not dead. Discarded, separated.

TINA: Like a divorce. With no lawyers to represent it.

BEN: A symbol of the narcissistic age!

TINA: Her girlfriend too? Her girlfriend admires you too?

BEN: Both of them do. "Your dad's cool," she says. He's everywhere. Wooow. "He's famous."

TINA: Unlike me.

BEN: Of course, unlike you.

TINA: Don't they like me? Is that it?

BEN: You seem a little irrelevant.

TINA: Irrelevant?

BEN: Since you don't do anything.

TINA: I have my activities, my friends, and my cultural events blog. I comment on everything on Facebook and I always return a "Like." Plus I have the magazine project with Adele.

BEN: Your magazine isn't a project, sweetheart, it's a fantasy.

TINA: We're searching for a groundbreaking idea!

BEN: For three years? Searching for an idea?

TINA: Ideas are tricky. They duck, they dodge, they deceive you.

BEN: Maybe ideas think you're a bit retarded.

TINA: That's why my daughter doesn't like me?

BEN: And because you call me shit.

TINA: I don't call you shit. I'm just quoting the world!

BEN: The internet is not the world.

TINA: What is then?

BEN: For starters, the world begins with your daughter and her girlfriend.

TINA: (*Defeated*) Did they sleep together again last night?

BEN: Most likely.

TINA: If they'd just let me know. That woman is a legal adult. And at night you can hear the screaming and groaning! Yuck!

BEN: Let them be.

TINA: You should ask for an explanation. Make a rule or something.

BEN: Like what?

TINA: Like they can't sleep together without permission.

BEN: That's not going to work. And they'll do it anyway.

TINA: Like they can't have sex in the room right below our bathroom…

BEN: (*Looking at the floor*) We could drill two holes right here and spy on them.

TINA: That's not funny. You have to make them see that they need to respect other people. How can they be so inconsiderate? Don't they care that we're here, right above them?

BEN: Sweetheart, you're living in the wrong era.

TINA: Is that it? I'm the one who's wrong?

BEN: No one worries about other people anymore. These days, if it's not you, it's invisible.

TINA: I'm not invisible!

BEN: So you think they care if you hear them having sex?

TINA: Of course not.

BEN: Then you're invisible to them.

TINA: Just, say something to them, please.

BEN: Why don't you say something?

TINA: I will when she starts talking to me again.

BEN: She's still mad at you?

TINA: Not at me. At my sense of humor.

BEN: Yeah well, sometimes your sense of humor and your opinions are hard to tell apart.

TINA: Really? (*Tina turns her back on him. Ben watches her in the mirror. She laughs. He goes to her.*) It was just a joke…

BEN: A bit insensitive, admit it.

TINA: You think? "In a lesbian relationship, which woman makes the sandwiches? Answer: neither, because they both eat each other."

(They both laugh, trying to keep it down.)

BEN: Ok, I admit. I thought it was really funny.

TINA: But she…

BEN: She didn't take it that way.

TINA: She gets mad over everything. A week ago I heard her girlfriend say practically the same thing. And you should've heard how hard she laughed!

BEN: Quit turning this chapter of hers into a big deal. The girl won't last.

TINA: Are you sure?

BEN: It's a phase.

TINA: Why?

BEN: Because she knows it bothers us.

TINA: Exactly. It bothers us. Both of us.

BEN: You more.

TINA: Than you?

BEN: That's right.

TINA: Why? Because I'm the narrow-minded one?

BEN: No, but...

TINA: I don't like that girl. That's all. Her taste, her mannerisms, her culture...they're all different. I don't see myself being a grandmother to kids with her...

BEN: Color

TINA: Features.

BEN: That's all?

TINA: That's all.

BEN: Nothing else?

TINA: And she's driving a wedge between us, of course.

BEN: Jealousy?

TINA: You think Nicole might be mentally retarded in some way? I mean, she's got no sense of humor. You know that's a sign of stunted intelligence.

BEN: Our Nicole?

TINA: Sometimes I get that impression.

BEN: I don't think...

TINA: And here we did everything we could to make sure she was a genius.

BEN: That super-sperm bank cost an arm and a leg.

TINA: I remember that name, super-sperm, because it sounded like they meant sperm that came from Superman. We chose scientists and artists and nothing. I always had my doubts about that clinic, I told you... I mentioned it to Nicole.

BEN: You told Nicole you think the genius clinic cheated us with her?

TINA: Yeah, sure. Was that bad?

BEN: And then you ask why she's mad at you?

TINA: You think she's mad because I said she's dumb, not because of the homophobic joke?

BEN: Both! Your daughter thinks you're ignorant. How can you say things like that to her?

TINA: Why not?

BEN: Because you don't say things like that.

TINA: We should have the right to say whatever we want.

BEN: To say or to insult?

TINA: Both.

BEN: Insult the very thing we want to protect?

TINA: Protect at any cost? What for?

BEN: To be civilized? Modern? To save our species?

TINA: If you met the people in the grocery store, darling, you wouldn't think that was such a noble goal.

BEN: Someone's worth it. You, for instance.

TINA: I'm worth it?

BEN: Of course.

TINA: You're just saying that because you know hypocrites make me sick, right?

BEN: I'm telling you the truth.

TINA: Your generosity sucks.

BEN: It's not…

TINA: Remember Adele's niece?

BEN: The one who was born sick.

TINA: Delayed.

BEN: A bit older than Nicole.

TINA: Yeah, she's the reason we decided we wanted a genius baby.

BEN: Don't be cruel, it wasn't because of her…

TINA: I went to Adele's yesterday. The family was there, her niece too. At one point, we all stopped talking because she was going to play the flute. I was surprised, but I didn't say anything. I thought, she's going to play the flute? There's a shocker. But the thing is, her playing was atrocious. Horrific. Some other instrument might not have sounded so bad. But…the flute? When it was over everyone clapped and shouted bravo, how pretty. They even went on about how she composed it herself! I was one second away from standing up and saying: seriously? Do we really have to be so tolerant of the fallen? That's what I'm saying to you now: do you have to treat me this way?

BEN: No, of course not.

TINA: Don't forget it.

BEN: It's a good thing you didn't say anything to Adele about her niece and the flute.

TINA: Why?

BEN: Because she's your only friend.

TINA: So?

BEN: So she'd hate you.

TINA: Like Nicole and her girlfriend.

BEN: Exactly.

TINA: Why?

BEN: Because it's offensive.

TINA: Are we or aren't we free to express our opinions?

BEN: No. We're not. Not all of them.

TINA: Because there they are, ready to slap you with their political correctness!

BEN: It's their way to rebel.

TINA: By converting to Puritanism! Moralists! Hypocrites! Fundamentalists!

(We hear a noise in the distance)

BEN: What was that?

TINA: The crocodile?

BEN: Is that what crocodiles sound like?

TINA: I think they sound like... *(She makes a crocodile noise, however she wants.)*

BEN: No, that's like a lion. I think crocodiles sound like...

(They both make noises replaying the gestures and movements of the preceding dialogue. They repeat it several times. Laughing at first. But then serious, as if they had been transported back to a time in prehistory. Then, another noise joins in. They both fall silent.)

TINA: It sounds like...scratching.

BEN: You think it's trying to get in the house?

TINA: An alligator in the house!

BEN: Let me hear!

(Absolute silence. We hear nothing. But they hear it.)

BEN: Did you hear that?

TINA: Loud and clear. It's frightening. *(Facing the audience)* That thing is terrifying me!

(Ben goes to his side of the bathroom. He pulls out what looks like a shaving kit, but inside is a gun.)

BEN: Don't worry, Tina, I won't let it in the house.

TINA: But Ben, crocodiles have bullet-proof skin!

BEN: No skin is bullet-proof. Bullets go through anything natural. Elephants, tigers, crocodiles. Lizards!

TINA: How do you know?

BEN: I've seen how they kill them.

TINA: Where?

BEN: On TV.

TINA: And TV's enough?

BEN: Of course. One shot in the neck and those things slink into the water and disappear.

TINA: There's no water here for it to swim off and let us be.

BEN: *(Showing her)* I've got nine bullets and twenty more in the box.

TINA: And you know how to shoot that thing?

BEN: No, I don't. But, how hard can it be? If any vertebrate mammal can do it, I guess I can too.

TINA: Yeah, but how?

BEN: You point, pull this and...

(We hear two gunshots. The two get the fright of their lives, but shush each other. Ben tries to get rid of the gun, but sets it on Tina's side of the counter. She pushes it to Ben's side with her iPad. The shots went through the bathroom floor, leaving two holes. She covers them with a bathroom rug.)

TINA: So no one will see.

BEN: I don't know how it went off!

TINA: Nicole must think I finally put a bullet in you, two bullets.

BEN: You put a bullet in me?

TINA: Of course. I'm the one who's ignorant.

(They hear a siren approaching.)

BEN: They're coming.

TINA: A little late. I guess a crocodile on your doorstep isn't all that transcendental for city crime rates. Now if it were outside some celebrity's door! Go warn Nicole. So the dummy doesn't open the door to leave with that idiot and let the thing in to devour us all! *(Ben makes to leave. Tina stops him, pointing at the gun)* Shouldn't you hide that thing?

(Ben does. He leaves. But he comes back and kisses her. The kiss is unusual for them, like they were a couple of teenagers. Afterward, they look at each other like they don't recognize one another.)

BEN: Superwoman.

TINA: *(Humming the song, mocking the moment)* "B-B-B-Benny and the Jets…Oh but they're weird and they're wonderful…!"

(Annoyed, Ben leaves. Tina is alone. She looks around the bathroom. On the verge of laughter, she catches sight of the Hopper painting and stops. She makes a gesture of displeasure. She goes to the window, tripping over the rug covering the two bullet holes. She leans over a bit to look through the holes. Pauses. Sighs. Then

she goes to the window and makes the wild animal noise again, lizard-like.)

TINA: Idiotic crocodile, I'll show you how it's done! *(But something else grabs her attention)* There goes our girl, waiting for that perverted lover of hers to bite her... With all the animals out there, there go two more. And the biggest bitch of all, my daughter wrapped around her black lover in that hunk-of-junk red Corolla. You're leaving? You're not going to look back to see me? If I scream an insult, I bet you'll turn to look at me then! *(An idea occurs to Tina. She makes a phone call. While she's waiting for an answer, she growls like she was a crocodile.)* Adele, I've got it! The idea for our magazine. We should put it out weekly. In print, but online too. Family, religion, sex, race, immigration, issues that stir up outrage, anger, hate. And listen to the name I just came up with: The Viral Crocodile. *(Listens)* Because there's one outside my house. *(Listens)* Yes, a real crocodile. *(Listens)* I don't know, it must've escaped from the zoo. Anyway the thing is we're stuck in here waiting for the cops to come and I was talking to Ben, the kidnapper of video game music, my plagiarizing vampire of a husband who sucks other people's blood to stay alive, and it hit me: we'll do an outraged magazine. A magazine that will rip the mask off of puritans, moralists, hypocrites, and fundamentalists. And attack that cliché respect that's nothing but a way to fuck with our freedom to say whatever we want. We'll put an end to political correctness. We'll ridicule, yes, ridicule anyone who pretends they're civilized when the truth is they're hiding the animals they are. What do you think? I'm opening a Facebook account right now, Twitter, Instagram, the works, to see how the idea goes over! *(Begins opening accounts on social media sites from her iPad)* You don't like The Viral Crocodile? *(Listens)* The Viral Alligator? *(Listens)* The blood-sucking Vampire... The Viral Vampire! What do you think? *(Listens)* The

Viral Vampire! That's it! *(Working on her iPad)* That's what we'll call it. It's catchy. I can see the hashtags now. *(Enter Ben. Tina, to the phone)* See you tomorrow, Adele. Bye sweetie. *(Hangs up. To Ben)* How were the girls?

BEN: I don't...I think...they weren't in her room.

TINA: They went out?

BEN: How could they leave with that lizard at the door?

TINA: They must've gone out the back...

BEN: Did you see them?

(Somber music plays.)

TINA: Of course not. *(Taking pictures with her iPad from the window)* Come on, let's get a video of how terrified we are. I want to make it the magazine's first post!

BEN: The magazine?

TINA: The Viral Vampire. *(With her iPad, video)* "They left an alligator on the plagiarist's doorstep. This is not a simulation, this is real. A plagiarist kidnapped by wild animals."

BEN: No, wait, don't post that...Vampire?

TINA: *(Writing on her iPad)* We've got 50 followers already...!

BEN: If you're going to post on social media, please, don't use my name...

TINA: *(Writing on her iPad)* Twitter...

BEN: I want people to forget that music business…

TINA: *(Writing on her iPad)* "Should we build a wall to separate ourselves from the animals invading us?"

BEN: Maybe if I check myself into rehab.

TINA: *(Writing on her iPad)* Six people already shared it, in seconds!

BEN: Then they'll all feel sorry for me. And they'll forget, or forgive, which is the same thing…

TINA: *(Writing on her iPad, making it up)* "The animals have escaped from the zoo! The rhino's running wild, the leopard, elephants are chasing down our children…"

BEN: They'll see you're not a sicko, you're just very sick…

TINA: *(Writing on her iPad)* More than 500 retweets! And all signed by…

BEN: Like when a confused kid takes a gun to school…

TINA: *(Looking at him)* #ViralVampire

BEN: And gets some respect…

TINA: *(Writing on her iPad)* Can anyone see the similarity between a stampede of animals and a caravan of immigrants? *(To Ben)* And in just 88 characters.

BEN: It's not that we're narcissists…

TINA: *(Writing on her iPad)* Who can deny that middle class whites are running from a pack of wild animals? 78 characters.

BEN: We just have to be connected to everyone...

TINA: *(Writing on her iPad)* "We see animals running. Where's the wall? Where does terror begin?" 66 characters.

BEN: In that mundane interaction that make us so cruel.

TINA: *(Writing on her iPad)* Look! They're insulting me already! Incredible! I'm trending! This is great!

(Somber music ends.)

BEN: Welcome to the party.

TINA: *(Writing on her iPad)* Now I'll run with you.

BEN: Tina, no...

TINA: Vampire will speak!

BEN: You can't tell

TINA: What? You confessed?

BEN: I didn't confess anything!

TINA: Your crime

BEN: My crime?

TINA: Yes. That's right. *(Writing on her iPad)* You give us this day our daily crime.

BEN: Which is what exactly?

(Tina shoots him a defiant look. She types on her iPad furiously. Ben turns his back on her, defeated. The phone rings. Ben hesitates. Tina motions to him to answer.)

BEN: Tina, it's the police.

TINA: About the crocodile?

BEN: *(Ben nods. Talks to the phone)* Yes, we called about the animal. *(Ben leans to look out the window. Tina follows him. He listens)* We don't know where it came from. It's just here. An enormous, green lizard. A predator that could kill anyone passing by. *(Listens)* It's out in front of the house! Come up the driveway, but instead of going down the side head up the walkway. That's where the palm tree is and right next to it is the lizard, lying in front of the door. I can see it from here, officer! A massive lizard. *(Listens)* No, we don't know if it's angry. Lizards always look pissed off, I can tell you that much. *(Listens)* We weren't planning to ask if he felt strange walking around the neighborhood instead of swimming in his lake. We're talking about a filthy animal, you know? Do something, please! *(Listens)* What? *(To Tina)* You're out there right now?

(They both look out the window.)

TINA: I don't see anything...

(Suddenly, Ben gives a shout of raw, personal hatred, like he's drawing on all the outrage he's ever felt in his life.)

BEN: *(Listens, terrified)* What? *(Listens, terrified)* Oh my god, are you sure? *(Listens, terrified)* No, that's not possible!

TINA: *(Frightened)* What? What's going on?

BEN: *(Covers the mouthpiece)* The officer says the lizard is..! A stuffed animal!

TINA: What?

BEN: A stuffed animal. The monster is a stuffed animal!

TINA: A prank?

BEN: They already checked!

TINA: Bu…but…That size?

BEN: They say it belongs to the neighbor kid. He had it on his balcony and somehow it fell down here.

(Pause. They both look out the window, angry. Ben slams down the receiver. We hear the police over a megaphone: "False alarm" "Return to your homes" "It's nothing." Laughter.)

TINA: You see them laughing?

BEN: And playing with it.

TINA: They're mocking us. Mocking us.

BEN: That sarcasm, they're ridiculing us…

TINA: They're humiliating us.

BEN: Fucking cops.

TINA: Asshole neighbors.

BEN: Trash.

TINA: Intruders.

BEN: How do we get away?

TINA: How do we defend ourselves?

BEN: You have to draw your gun before they do.

TINA: Call a spade a spade.

BEN: Goddamn people.

TINA: Goddamn kid.

BEN: Goddamn crocodiles.

TINA: Goddamn stuffed animal city.

(We hear the chorus of Elton John's "Bennie and the Jets." Black out.)

3 /

(Again we see a video of Detective Pineda speaking into a microphone or recorder. The digital clock with large numbers reads 4:01 p.m.)

PINEDA: *(Off/Video)* Detective Jacinto Pineda, Homicide. Statement: case of the double murder of Nicole Galloway and Adriana Fuentes. Interview with Christina Galloway, mother of Nicole Galloway in the presence of her lawyer... *(Motions to the lawyer to state her name)*

LAWYER: *(Off/Video)* Mary Williams...

PINEDA: *(Off/Video)* Let's get started...

(When the lights come up onstage, we see Tina alone. Dimly we see Ben, in the bathroom, getting ready. The clock now reads 5:30 p.m.)

TINA: Problems with Nicole? The kind every mother of a teenage girl has. Sometimes we'd go without talking for days, over just about any little thing, but the big fights we patched up in minutes. *(Listens)* She'd been seeing our neighbor, the other girl, Adriana, for two months. *(Listens)* Of course I was surprised she liked someone... so black. But it never bothered me. Our family's very open-minded, no hang-ups, no prejudices. Modern. I understood her actually. It's not like men are so great they're the only ones you can fall in love with, right Detective Pineda? I always liked the girl, Adriana, and her family, the Fuentes, were wonderful neighbors. *(Short pause. She listens and answers.)*
We're getting divorced. It's nearly finalized. I mean, I'm just waiting for him to move out. We had no problem

dividing our assets. We'd left Nicole a trust fund, in case she showed up. *(Listens)* It was Ben's idea for me to keep the house.
(Short pause. She listens and answers.)
Nicole liked playing those simulation games her dad worked on. She was a fan of anything that implied living a life other than your own. A wish. That's it. Her wish was to be someone else: to go away, change her name, last, first, everything. In those sims she lived her life with a different name, different family, different problems. She idolized celebrities, technology, and herself most of all. Let's just say she was your run-of-the-mill 21st-century narcissist. I guess that comes from movies, the main character always showing how everything depends on one person. That's not true, but it's the message. That's simulation: everything depends on you. So we create our own world and only think about ourselves. In the end, other people disappear and there's less stress. Because no matter how bad you screw up your simulated life, you're always going to be better off there than in your real life. Getting fucked over in real life hurts. In real life, you don't control even your own breathing. And it's not even worth trying! Because the payoffs in real life are so few and so simple. In short, real life is a redundant hell, detective. You know.
(Listens. Stands.)
I think it all began with a Superman t-shirt. When I was little, I spent eleven months in the hospital, with this virus I caught. In the hospital, all I did was suffer, like everyone else: infections, operations, heart problems. I thought I'd never get out of there. Until this company gave us Superman t-shirts. And we loved them. Nothing like dying to make you believe in superheroes. Then, I started getting better. Yeah, of course, it was what the doctors expected, that I'd recover, but at six I figured that t-shirt had turned me into a superhero. Even though Mom explained over and over again: "the treatment, the medicine, and stop babbling about Superman because later you'll try to go flying out the window…" And of

course, I did. When they finally let me out of the hospital and I got home, I ran straight to my room, threw a towel over my shoulders, pulled on my brightest pair of panties, and shot to the window, ready to jump out and fly. Mom grabbed me just before I leapt into thin air. *(Listens)* How tall was I? *(Listens)* Oh, the building? I was 6 feet up, or less. Less. *(It's obvious she hears laughter)* I could've really hurt myself… *(Listens)* If I'd jumped head first, for example!
(Touches her shirt) Anyway, I'm a grown woman now, not six years old. Still, I'm not 100% convinced I'm not Supergirl. And if I leap into thin air maybe I can fly with that powerful t-shirt of mine. And no matter what happens, I won't get hurt. *(Listens)* We're on the first floor? Well, it's a figure of speech. Anyway, it's my Superman t-shirt that's always made me feel exceptional. Special. Original. Not like other people. *(She looks out at the audience and reveals the Superman t-shirt under her blouse. She laughs. Listens.)* Well, Detective Pineda, it's not that I think I'm amazing, but I am about to be gunned down by the enemies of the world. Doesn't that at least make me fascinating? *(What Pineda says makes her angry. She closes her blouse covering the t-shirt.)* The house? My husband, Ben, suggested I keep it. *(Listens)* Secrets? Me? Are you out of your mind? *(Stands up, leaving)* Don't you know who I am?

(Music. Today. Master bathroom in the Galloway house. 11 a.m. Ben is in the tub. He has his iPad beside him and a little further away, but still in reach, Tina's iPad. She stands at the mirror, in underwear.)

BEN: How do you think your people will react?

TINA: They'll be surprised.

BEN: Does Adele know anything?

TINA: Nothing.

BEN: You sure? She's your best friend.

TINA: I don't have a best friend.

BEN: Your ally at Vampire.

TINA: We agreed not to say anything to anyone.

BEN: I figured you'd make an exception.

TINA: None. Did you?

BEN: No. Of course not. I haven't told anyone.

TINA: The way we're doing it today is better.

BEN: All together.

TINA: Just one explanation.

BEN: No formalities.

TINA: And no conflicts.

BEN: No contradictions.

TINA: Once they're here, I'll get their attention and…

BEN: You'll tap on a glass.

TINA: Like a bell. Then, I'll go first, because you get all tongue-tied and start by saying you're sorry.

BEN: First Tina. Yes of course: you're the famous one.

TINA: Being famous has no bearing on this, Ben. We're announcing our divorce and absolute separation starting today. And asking, please, starting this August day, that they call us at different numbers…Cell, home, work…

BEN: Without asking us about the other.

TINA: Yes, that in particular.

BEN: Because we won't know a thing. Separated. Totally. What if they don't all come?

TINA: I called twenty of my closest people, including reporters and coworkers from Viral Vampire. If ten of them show, the whole world will know in seconds. *(Tina goes to the toilet. She sees the Hopper poster and remembers. Sitting on the toilet)* Don't forget to put the poster on the list of things I'm keeping!

BEN: What poster?

TINA: The Hopper

BEN: On my list?

TINA: On mine, moron.

BEN: Yours? Are you sure?

TINA: I adore that painting. Three weeks ago we agreed I could keep it. Right?

BEN: But…

TINA: Are you having second thoughts?

BEN: You know it's a poster, that's all?

TINA: What's it called?

BEN: From the Museum in Osaka…

TINA: The painting. You remember the name?

BEN: Eleven A.M. The August…

TINA: Feeling. The August Feeling. I love it. I want it.

BEN: Honestly I didn't know you liked it. It's been there forever. You hardly ever looked at it. It was a decoration, that's all.

TINA: *(Serious)* Is something wrong?

BEN: Whatever you say. *(Ben checks his iPad but doesn't find what he's looking for)* Where's the latest division of assets?

TINA: On my iPad.

(Ben picks it up. Tina does her business while checking the web on her phone.)

BEN: In Notes?

TINA: Aha.

BEN: Did you change the passcode?

TINA: Every day.

BEN: To keep me from seeing your secrets?

TINA: You or anybody.

BEN: You mean the people who want to kill you? So they don't find your Vampire mysteries?

TINA: I'm not worried about those people.

BEN: True: they only want to murder you.

TINA: Yeah, but they're nobodies.

BEN: Well then so am I, sweetheart.

TINA: You never know.

BEN: Tina, today may be the last day of our life together; today we may be telling the whole world; this blazing divorce may finally be absolute, but you and I will always be synchronized.

TINA: Like clocks.

BEN: No matter what, I will always be someone to you. *(Shouts)* Code!!!

TINA: 4948

BEN: *(Types on the iPad)* There, Hopper's included as one of your most prized possessions. Now every woman's going to wish she could divorce a guy like me.

TINA: Why do you always say yes?

BEN: Because I never say no.

TINA: I expected more of a battle.

BEN: Why?

TINA: Sometimes men see divorce as a war that sums up all their defeats. Out of a desire for victory, for just one in their whole life, they treat the divorce like a battle to the death. It's not about the assets, or the kids: it's about victory.

BEN: Anything else?

TINA: *(Typing on her phone)* Just a sec, this is important...

(Ben leans forward to see her from the tub. To him the picture is unforgettable: Tina on the toilet, typing as fast as she can on her phone, popping up and down, like a reflex.)

BEN: Sharing the bathroom this way was fine when we were married, Tina. But now it feels like taking things too far. Did you really have to come do your business while I was in the tub?

TINA: It saves time. It's not personal.

BEN: Personal? You're pissing or shitting with the door wide open, jumping up, cleaning the wax out of your ears, blowing your nose, I don't know, your most private stuff, in front of me!

TINA: Does it bother you?

BEN: If we still loved each other, you wouldn't dare!

TINA: You want me to close the door? Is that it?

BEN: No, no, no. You're just a wild animal, that's all. A beast.

TINA: Beasts like me aren't personal, chéri. We save time. In an hour, twenty guests will be coming for what they think is an informative meeting on the highly publicized case of Nicole and her friend, but...

BEN: By the way, I thought I'd say a few words about that...

TINA: There's no need. They get all that on the web. Now our news...

BEN: The divorce...

TINA: That they don't see coming.

BEN: They're about to get a real shock.

TINA: See? And it's going down in 60 minutes. And I haven't had a bath and I'm not dressed. And you, you're just sitting there soaking. If we get ready together, we'll have time for coffee after, and a bite to eat. We can check the news, our mail, the latest tweets. One more hour together isn't going to confuse us.

BEN: Seeing you do your things on the toilet is confusing, Tina.

TINA: Why?

BEN: Because it makes you look human. Like all the ugly things they say about you just disappear when you shit or piss.

TINA: You're a real charmer.

BEN: Don't forget it. If you ever need to see yourself as a person, count on me to hang around while you do your nastiness.

TINA: Thanks a lot. You're a real prince of filth. But that won't be necessary. Divorce is divorce.

BEN: So we really won't see each other at all?

TINA: We might. Around. Maybe, by chance. But we'll eye each other like two animals that once fought over the same prey.

BEN: Who now stare each other down and remember…

TINA: When they did filthy things face to face.

BEN: When they saw a view…or Hopper's painting and remembered what it was to be a pack, the thrill of the fight. The August Feeling: when they loved each other and life had meaning…

TINA: But now reliving what they were and what they did is disgusting.

BEN: Disgusting.

TINA: Like a toilet. Disgusting.

BEN: Quite an idea, my sweet vampire.

(When Tina stands up from the toilet and is about to flush, Ben leaps from the tub as though electrocuted. He strides toward her, nude, splashing water everywhere.)

BEN: No, wait!

TINA: *(Frightened, looking toward the window)* What's going on?

BEN: Don't flush!

TINA: Why? Is it broken? Is there a bomb?

BEN: Don't do it!

TINA: You're getting dirty water all over the bathroom!

(Ben sits on the toilet.)

BEN: Ready!

DIVORCE

TINA: What on earth are you doing?

(Ben does his business too. She watches, waiting for him to give a credible and reasonable answer. He waits a beat and then realizes he has to say something.)

BEN: I want our filth to be together one last time!

(Tina turns away, annoyed.)

TINA: Jesus Christ, you're such a pig!

BEN: This will be their final journey together!

TINA: Why do you have to be so repulsive?

BEN: Because I can.

TINA: You're an animal!

(Tina walks to the middle of the bathroom. She picks up Ben's iPad by mistake.)

BEN: That's mine, gorgeous. Yours is…

(She reads what's on screen.)

TINA: Divorce
Once, two spoons in bed,
now tined forks
Across the granite table
and the knives they have hired
What's this?

BEN: A poem. Billy Collins.

TINA: Filth, scum, plagiarism and now poetry. You're not going gay on me now? Are you?

BEN: Billy Collins is very well-known. He was Poet Laureate…

TINA: We ran a piece in Vampire about middle-aged men who go gay after a divorce. It was a huge hit. We offended nearly everyone. It's still trending online. Maybe you're like them, huh? Fashionably gay?

(Ben flushes the toilet and stares at her.)

BEN: *(To the toilet)* There they go. Together. Embarking on their secret journey.

TINA: A divorced man who's gone to the homosexual side of the moon. You could get married again.

BEN: Get married?

TINA: To a man, of course.

BEN: *(Takes a towel and wraps it around himself. Suddenly serious)* Tina, we'll still be friends. Won't we?

TINA: What?

BEN: Are we friends?

TINA: *(Pitying)* I was mocking you, but I wasn't serious.

BEN: Mocking someone is serious.

TINA: Of course we're friends.

BEN: Then we should be nice to each other.

TINA: But none of that kissing and saying how pretty, how beautiful you look, or oh how well you play the flute, right?

BEN: Just what's normal. Polite. Decent.

TINA: That all depends.

BEN: On what?

TINA: On who you're seeing, for instance.

BEN: I'm not seeing anyone, Tina.

TINA: I mean if you were dating another woman, or another man...I mean, would you tell me?

BEN: I would tell you. I'm not seeing anyone.

TINA: Not even Burrito?

BEN: Narito?

TINA: Your assistant.

BEN: She's not my assistant, Tina. I'm not working. I was blacklisted by every company. Plagiarism... remember?

TINA: That doesn't mean you might not call your little burro or that she won't come braying up behind you and spread your back legs, all slit eyed and floppy eared with desire.

BEN: Nari Ok doesn't work with me, she's married and has two kids!

TINA: Then that other woman!

BEN: What other woman?

TINA: Narito!

BEN: There is no Narito!

TINA: She's thinking about you anyway!

BEN: No one is thinking about me!

TINA: (*Serious*) Ben, all I ask is that you don't start seeing anyone right away. Because you know how people are...Our friends will say that's why we got divorced. That we were hiding it. That the whole mutual boredom thing is bullshit, just like the stress over the death threats, or living with cops, or the ludicrous amount of attention I get. That your parody in a rehab center for plagiarists was fake. That even the discovery of Nicole and her girlfriend's brutally murdered bodies, in our own backyard, had nothing to do with our divorce. No, instead they'll say the reason for our unexpected news is the oldest one in the book: you found a younger woman. That's what the merciless blogs and Vampire's enemies will say. They'll turn me into a viral laughingstock, with keyboard cat playing and singing a song about middle-aged women replaced by Japanese and Chinese music students; teenagers flipping cute little signs one after the other begging old women like me to leave their daddies alone. You know how the internet loves a downfall, the price of mockery. And when the viral video loses steam, they'll finish me off with the low blow; princesses dressed up and singing Disney tunes, confessing that Tina, ex-Galloway, ex-Superwoman, the post-special, post-exceptional and post-viral Scrooge, has some congenital defect, some contagious disease, something that only divorced women get. They'll do it, Ben. And I can't take it. I'd rather have the Kalashnikovs!

BEN: But that's exactly what you do to everyone else with Vampire!

TINA: That's why, I know what I'm talking about.

(Ben takes Tina's iPad again.)

BEN: Don't worry. I'll put it on the list. Under the dresser, the recliner, Hopper's August Feeling, the impossibility of love.

TINA: Don't write love, put down sex. I'm sick of love. I don't want to hear one more word about it till I'm reborn as a rock in the depths of the ocean.

BEN: Sex. *(Types)* Preferably with cops?

TINA: The cops I like aren't protecting me anymore. They're gone. Ever since they found Nicole in the backyard it seems like they're hoping they'll kill me too. *(Getting an idea)* Maybe they should kill you the same way! As long as they're here. After all, you were a man people hated. And the worst kind: a loser who isn't even on social media anymore.

(Ben goes to her, slowly. He looks like he's going to kiss her. But he touches her bare arm. She looks at his crotch, to see if he's aroused, but sees nothing. She gestures "What do you want?")

TINA: Do you really have to touch me?

BEN: I want our affection to be private, Tina. Between us, personal. Like when you're having a beer with friends and no one's looking at a screen, they're all drinking in the words of the occasion. Like we could talk in an original moment, one that's unrepeatable, un-digital. Just us, in the instant, uncontainable, live, no furious replicas, no insults, no selfies, no likes, no sharing with people who've never been with us. The way it used to be: passionate people without spreading, or amplifying, or documenting the experience. Eight hidden wineglasses, untouched by the virtual, destined for secrecy, fellowship, and oblivion without leaving a trace. The way it was back when a net was just an object to save us from falling.

(Tina takes his face between her hands. She kisses his forehead.)

TINA: Ben, sweet Ben, sweetheart, darling. There's one truth. And this is it: that's all gone. There are no originals, no mysteries. *(She lets go of Ben and goes to her iPad.)* I'm going to check my tweets. I've been offline for like five whole minutes. *(She says the last part with a sarcasm that makes Ben laugh.)*

BEN: Less than five minutes, Tina, don't exaggerate!

TINA: Five minutes worth of tweets was all it took to topple seven governments in the Arab spring, darling.

(Ben goes to the sink. He picks up his razor and pretends he's going to slit his throat with it. Tina doesn't see, since she's focused on her iPad.)

TINA: *(Checking online)* Let's see: the usual enemies… Our post on people who hope to get their heart crushed was popular. A fantastic piece by Adele… People who hate us en masse, newcomers, has-beens. Memes about me…Here's a really funny one. They photoshopped me with a chimp girl. And they call me…that… the usual… Our enemies have no imagination, darling. There's no creativity in swearing anymore. They should learn from Vampire… How many times do you think I've popped up in the last few seconds? Woooow! Five tweets a second with my name! What do you think?

BEN: That cats are just as popular.

TINA: Don't you think that's a surprising number?

BEN: Too many people spending too much time and effort on thinking up nonsense and then saying it out loud.

TINA: No one's talking about thinking, chéri. It's about echoing.

BEN: It's the web, Tina. Everything's on it.

TINA: No, not everything. For example, there's not much on you. (*Types on her iPad*) How many people are talking about you these days? I type in "plagiarism" on Google and click search. Maybe you pop up first. Maybe you have seven tweets a second.

BEN: The dregs of Vampire's first post, if you recall.

TINA: You shouldn't complain. When we made you viral you got hashtagged, viewed and retweeted for up to seven days straight. 1,567 likes on Facebook in two days.

BEN: And it turned me to shit.

TINA: As I recall, you already were shit.

BEN: Thanks: you and your nostalgia.

TINA: Don't blame me. You know Viral Vampire doesn't hold back. That's what it's about. Saying everything.

BEN: (*Agitated*) Everything? Saying everything?

TINA: What is, what will be and what should be.

BEN: (*Turns to look at her, angry*) For fuck's sake, Tina: quit your self-indulgent monologuing. You're ignorant but you know what's going on and you know your magazine is...

TINA: The sign of the times. The champion of freedom.

BEN: And they call you...

TINA: Tina, defender of the West! Superwoman! Bulletproof skin! Look what they're saying online: J'suis Vampire! Avatars: J'suis Vampire! Search engines: J'suis Vampire! Even Google did a Doodle that says...J'suis Vampire!

(Ben explodes and throws his iPad at her. It falls in the tub. Tina is terrified, like a baby fell in the water. Ben, losing it.)

BEN: A horrid rag, Tina! The symbol of bad taste and contempt for others! A weekly dose of narcissism, arrogance, and prejudice that brags about truths it never reveals! That it doesn't know! I'm positive you don't know! I've lived with you! I know how ignorant you are!

TINA: I'm not ignorant!

BEN: How do you know? How do you know you're not ignorant?

TINA: Because they want to kill me!

BEN: That's why! Because you're a cretin! An imbecile! You and your magazine insulting everyone: Muslims, immigrants, minorities, blacks, socialists, conservatives, everyone but insults themselves! Because, no, no sir, that's freedom! Insults are sacred! Insults are an animal's most cherished right! Humiliation is freedom!

TINA: We're fighting the Man! Standing up to people too scared to hear the truth, people who hide behind pity, behind political correctness!

BEN: It's not politically correct! It's correct, period!

TINA: So I'm the bad guy because I tell people the truth?

BEN: The truth?

TINA: Yes, of course! The truth!

BEN: The Vampire truth!

TINA: The hidden truth!

BEN: The truth you decree!

TINA: Because it's true! Check online: everyone's with me! Everyone hates the people who want to kill me! The world's given me its stamp of approval!

BEN: Because they don't know you!

TINA: The way you do?

BEN: Because they don't know who you are!

TINA: And you do?

BEN: Because they love to think you stand for who they are!

TINA: Exactly: what they hide out of fear, out of hypocrisy. Who they really are, that's me!

BEN: Animals!

TINA: *(Shouts)* The terrorists won't win!

BEN: Well I'd say, thanks to you, they're doing great!

TINA: *(Moving away)* Whatever!

BEN: Admit it: the world would be much better off without your Viral Vampire!

TINA: Better, but less free!

BEN: Freedom of humiliation, mockery, destruction!

TINA: Equality for everyone!

BEN: No, not everyone!

TINA: Vampire's very democratic: our attacks are indiscriminate!

BEN: On people you choose! At your convenience!

TINA: No one's safe!

BEN: Especially people who share your prejudices!

TINA: I'm not prejudiced!

BEN: You show how arbitrary you are!

TINA: We show what's disgusting!

BEN: You publicize what's painful!

TINA: And everyone's better off because of it!

BEN: But, why?

TINA: Because I can!

BEN: Yes, but, why?

TINA: Because that's how I live!

BEN: Live on what? Attention? Power?

TINA: Money, preferably.

BEN: That's where it comes from? Cash for contempt?

TINA: What you're getting in the divorce, what you've been living on for five years now. Viral equals dollars, asshole!

BEN: *(Ben looks at her, disbelieving)* But... How?

TINA: And you thought I was ignorant when you don't understand what this is all about? This is a necessary service, sweetie. And we can provide it. *(Tries to put on lipstick)* A scandal because someone needs today's headline to disappear fast, to drop out of the spotlight. People desperate in their demand that tomorrow no one will be talking about them because they'll all be talking about the doctor who cut off the baby's wienie thinking it was the umbilical cord. *(Stops putting on lipstick)* "Circumcision by the hand of God." Some people say it was deliberate. They talk about the doctor's militant religion. Voluntary carelessness? *(Tries to put on lipstick)* And everyone up in arms: doctors offended, patients outraged, Jews mocked. The web red hot, the whole world firing off opinions. *(Stops putting on lipstick)* And at midnight, when keyboards are flaming with the neutered baby, flooded with memes of his wienie jumping like a bloody little worm, and everyone cruel, cruel, so cruel, worse than me and Vampire, cruel, incorrect, all of you cruel and laughing all while basking in your indignation, reveling in it, then a question pops up, a little question, buried in a post no one reads or sees: do you remember the corruption scandal that was trending first thing this morning?

BEN: And the end result?

TINA: *(Throws her lipstick at the mirror)* The most controversial magazine in English, the most successful and one of the most viral magazines in the world!

BEN: And you, condemned to death!

TINA: Condemned? Everyone's moved by the threats against Viral Vampire! There's no condemning. The world sees this is no less than an attack on freedom of speech.

BEN: That may be now, because before the threats and attacks, they despised you for your bad taste, your banality, your ignorance, your ability to offend everyone, your arrogance and your contempt for the weakest among us! Before they used to call you a fascist in 0.022 tweet seconds!

TINA: But now killing me is killing all of us! Vampire is many!

BEN: Some people are even questioning if the threats and attacks are real!

TINA: And if anyone doesn't agree with Viral Vampire it's because they support terrorism!

BEN: I swear: the one they fertilized with super sperm was you, not Nicole.

TINA: A little genius must have stayed in my blood.

BEN: Fine. That means when they bump you off with their Kalashnikovs, you'll replace the inconvenient news of the day too. How long will you be trending, #Tinavampirefullofholes?

TINA: Four days.

BEN: Long enough for someone to sleep easy with the crimes they committed.

TINA: That's what we're here for. And when you collect your fee, don't spend it all on one porn site.

(The phone rings. Tina thinks it's hers, but shakes her head. She points to Ben's, which has been sitting on a dresser. Ben answers.)

TINA: *(Looking at the bath tub)* Remember you killed your iPad by throwing it in the water. You know you lost everything on it?

BEN: (Covering the receiver) I have the Cloud. *(Talks on the phone)* Detective Pineda. *(Tina freezes. Listens)* I'll tell her. *(To Tina)* Detective Pineda's on his way over. He'll be here in a few minutes. He wants to know if you'll see him.

TINA: What's Pineda want now?

BEN: To talk to you.

TINA: Again?

BEN: He has some questions for you.

TINA: I don't know why. The first interview went really well.

BEN: I don't think he's convinced. He said something…

TINA: About what?

BEN: Accusations.

TINA: There weren't any accusations!

BEN: Police, when they repeat questions, it means…

TINA: What question?

BEN: The one about who got the house. Since the girls were buried in the backyard…

TINA: We didn't know they were there!

BEN: Right, but…

TINA: Someone killed them and hid them in our backyard. I made it clear they needed to investigate her horrid girlfriend's immigrant family, who by the way swore they'd seen the girls in Florida. You told me so yourself! Or isn't that true? I always figured she'd left the country, that Nicole had run away from home.

BEN: Because she hated us, that's what you told the Detective.

TINA: I didn't tell him. And she didn't hate me!

BEN: You more than me.

TINA: That's all in your head.

BEN: It was Detective Pineda who suggested the thing about…

TINA: He didn't suggest anything.

BEN: I think he did.

TINA: The gunshots? You mean the gunshots? That went off that day? That was you! When you were trying to defend me from the stuffed crocodile that was going to kill us all? Remember?

BEN: I explained and they don't match...

TINA: What? What doesn't match?

BEN: The bullets, my gun, they don't match anything.

TINA: So? What? What?

BEN: Well, maybe you...

TINA: I what?

BEN: I mean, the family's always the first suspect and...

TINA: Suspect of what?

BEN: When the detective asked that question...

TINA: Which one? Which question, Ben?

BEN: About when you saw Nicole out the window.

TINA: And I answered that fucking detective. Of course I answered him!

BEN: Truthfully?

TINA: As straightforward as possible.

BEN: But one thing needs clearing up.

TINA: Nothing needs clearing up!

BEN: Like there were...

TINA: What? There were what?

BEN: Secrets.

TINA: I don't have any secrets!

BEN: Of course you have secrets!

TINA: You put that in their heads!

BEN: That you have secrets! And the police want you to tell them!

TINA: Well then I'll demand to have a lawyer present! I have five lawyers at Vampire trained in civil rights, democracy, and freedom of speech, and they'll defend me the same way they've defended our right to say whatever we want without caring who feels implicated, injured, mocked or whatever! Let's see what the cops do with the knives I hired! That fucking detective Pineda won't screw me!

BEN: You'll have to tell him that.

TINA: I will. In private and online. I'll make it viral. Pineda better watch out. Vampire gets as many as five trends going every day on social media! Just let those goddamn cops try… let them try to fight my freedom of…!

BEN: That sounds dangerous in the middle of a double murder investigation.

TINA: They're not investigating me for double murder!

BEN: He wants to ask you…

TINA: What's he asking? What's that goddamn cop asking and with what right?

BEN: About the last time you saw Nicole.

(Now Tina really explodes, more than at any other point. She lets out a scream that reminds us of the lizard in Act Two. She goes to her iPad and slams it against the sink as many as fifteen times, screaming.)

TINA: My right...my right to be...to say...my freedom....they want to take it all...because of those goddamn... goddamn... fucking... moralists...!!!! *(She shatters the iPad. Then, she calms down. She takes Ben's towel off, leaving him naked. She uses it to dry herself. Finally, she sighs. Ben gets another towel and wraps it around himself before she begins her next text.)* Fine. Five years ago, August 12th at 11 a.m., my daughter Nicole left the house in her yellow dress, carrying her black and white striped backpack. She walked right by a terrible crocodile that was all set to devour us but turned out to be a stuffed animal. Nicole didn't pay any attention to it, maybe because she knew the animal was harmless...dead... right. Dead, harmless and stuffed. She got in a Toyota Corolla driven by her eighteen-year-old black girlfriend. She didn't look back at the house, much less at her mother. I, honestly, never saw her again.

BEN: And when they ask you: what did you do when you found out she had disappeared?

TINA: Two days later I called the police. Then a couple of bored cops showed up. Another teenager who up and leaves her parents? The stuffed animal's daughter, I think they said. Fill out this form, ma'am, they ordered me, and I heard them laugh. When I asked them what was so funny, they apologized. Turns out they were watching a video on one of their phones. Something with a dog jumping a fence. Something ridiculous. Then I realized. Other people are dead. Other people are unnecessary. The worst thing is being like other people.

BEN: You remember it that clearly?

TINA: And I'll tack on: I want to make it clear that my daughter was my whole life. My love for Nicole is the only love I ever had. When they found her body in the backyard of our house I didn't act surprised because the pain swept away my shock. The pain I felt when I knew for sure she was dead. And that, somehow, I had died with her. And I cried. I cried so hard that nobody heard me. To this day. I'll record that. And I'll put it on the web.

BEN: It'll go viral.

TINA: Of course it will. And it'll last. YouTube has tear-filled confessions that have stayed at the top for as long as ten years. With forty, fifty million views. More than even Taylor Swift's music videos. People watch them like it happened yesterday!

(The phone rings again.)

BEN: *(Looking at the cell phone screen)* It's Pineda.

TINA: Tell him we'll see him.

BEN: *(Ben answers)* Yes, she's ready to talk to you.

TINA: The lawyer...

BEN: By the way, Tina asked me to tell you that from now on any questions will be with her lawyers present. *(Listen)* Right, lawyers, plural. *(Listens)* It's not that we don't want to help with the investigation. This is about our daughter, as you know. The lawyers are to ensure we don't cause ourselves any problems. *(Listens)* No, we don't have problems. But we don't want to cause them. So you can't manipulate us into saying what we don't mean! You know my wife shapes public opinion, right? And that public opinion topples governments. *(Listens)* Well, you're government. *(Listens a long time. He gets a little nervous)* I see. We'll be here. *(Hangs up)* The detective didn't like the lawyer idea.

TINA: He doesn't have to like it.

BEN: He said that's how guilty people act.

TINA: We're not guilty.

BEN: Of course not. He said they've figured out it wasn't a crime of passion. That whoever did it really didn't care much.

TINA: Really?

BEN: They didn't care much.

TINA: So, like us.

(Tina is going to leave but stops at the tub.)

TINA: You think I have time to wash up?

BEN: A shower?

TINA: A bath.

BEN: It'll take longer to drain the water and fill it up again...

TINA: With what's in there.

BEN: In my dirty bathwater?

(Tina starts to undress.)

TINA: It's what I've been doing for the last 20 years.

BEN: You're a beast, you know?

TINA: It's natural.

BEN: You mean it's animal.

TINA: Human beings are animals.

(Tina gets in the tub. Happy. Ben turns away, disgusted.)

BEN: Enjoy.

TINA: It's still warm.

(Tina submerges herself completely and comes right back up. We see her swallow some of the water.)

TINA: Divine.

(They look at each other. Tina laughs at the surprise on Ben's face. He takes off his towel and is completely nude too.)

BEN: I'm swimming in your filth too.

(Ben gets in the tub. The water spills over. Now we see it is brown, filthy, nearly black.)

BEN: You're disgusting, Tina

TINA: You know what? Out of all my fabulous decisions, the best, or the second best, was divorcing you.

BEN: What was the best?

(She smells the water.)

TINA: Hey, by the way, this filthy bathwater of yours doesn't smell half bad.

BEN: Now that's the only thing you've said this morning that makes any sense.

(They look at each other, sitting side by side, naked in the bathtub.)

TINA: And here we are.

BEN: Like two pendulums.

TINA: Synchronized.

BEN: We can call this the September feeling, once everyone else has been eliminated.

TINA: You are my solitude.

BEN: And you're my bulletproof skin.

(They kiss.)

TINA: Hand me my pills.

BEN: Are you in pain?

TINA: Of course not.

BEN: Can I have a couple?

TINA: They're 500 mg.

BEN: Then give me three.

(They take the pills.)

TINA: *(Sighs. After a beat)* What you think she's doing now?

BEN: It doesn't matter anymore, Tina.

TINA: That's why I asked.

BEN: What?

TINA: What you think she's doing now.

BEN: Dancing. Nicole hasn't stopped dancing.

TINA: With that girl?

BEN: With all the girls. She's dancing with all the girls.

(After a while she leans in and licks his neck, savoring him.)

TINA: You taste like my filth.

(They splash each other, like a couple of kids. The clock reads 12 p.m. and the water is definitively black. Black out.)

THE END

GUSTAVO OTT

Gustavo Ott (Caracas, Venezuela). Playwright, novelist, participant in the International Writing Program at the University of Iowa (1993); Residence Internationale Aux Recollets in Paris (2006); and Cité Internationale des Arts de Paris Residency (2010). Chosen for the New Work Now! at the Joseph Papp Public Theater as well as for the Playwriting Program of La Mousson D'Ete at the Comedie Française. Recipient of numerous playwriting awards, including the Tirso de Molina International Playwriting Prize (Spain, 1998) and the Ricardo López Aranda International Playwriting Award (Spain, 2003). Nominated for The Helen Hayes/Charles MacArthur Award for Outstanding New Play or Musical (2009). Prix Ville de Paris/Etc_Caraïbe 2009 for Mademoiselle et Madame (Miss & Madame); FATEX Award for Playwriting (Merida, Spain, 2012). Finalist in the Metlife/Repertorio Español Nuestras Voces National Playwriting Competition (New York, 2011); Third BID Award "Hispanics in USA" (2010) for "Juanita Claxton" ; Aguijón Theater's Second International Hispanic Playwriting Award sponsored by the Cervantes Institute (Chicago, 2017) for "Brutality" and I Trasnocho Playwriting Award (Caracas, 2017) for *The Photo*.

HEATHER L. McKAY

Translator of Latin American and Spanish theater. A graduate of the MFA Translation Program at the University of Iowa, Heather has translated a wide range of authors, including Lope de Vega, Miguel de Cervantes, Federico García Lorca, Gustavo Ott, Augustín Moreto, Patricia Suárez, Jordi Casanovas, Marcelo Rodriguez, Ernesto Caballero, and Edén Coronado. Her translations have been staged, read and used for subtitling in New York, Washington, D.C., Atlanta, Dallas and in theaters around the U.S. Her translations can be found in *Spectacular Bodies, Dangerous Borders* (LATR Books); several anthologies, such as *International Plays for Young Audiences* (Meriwether); and *Plays and Prejudice; The Lipstick Plays; The Perversity Plays; The Catastrophe Plays, The Photo* and *Divorcées, Evangelists and Vegetarians (Magotts)*.

Made in the USA
Middletown, DE
21 July 2018